Mac D:

Private

Investigator

Tony McFadden

ISB: 978-0-6456733-5-7

DEDICATION

For Readers, everywhere.

You keep consuming, and I'll keep creating. Deal?.

ACKNOWLEDGMENTS

Many thanks to my acting friends in Perth who read the original screenplay upon which this is based. You brought it to life for me. Thanks Ron, Sue, Callum, Cathy, Dan and any others I may have missed..

Chapter One

It had been over a week since I saw a morning early enough for breakfast. A long but ultimately fruitful stakeout had closed a case that had taken a week of nights to bring to a resolution. I was in danger of becoming permanently nocturnal. I was seriously considering changing my name to Vlad.

It was early August. That time of year in Australia when the nights are cold, but the daytime is glorious. I had parked myself at The Pelican, a waterfront cafe miles from Sydney, both geographically and spiritually. Not that I had a spiritual bone in my body. I couldn't even commit fully to Atheism. I had escaped the smoke and ended up, not entirely by choice, about halfway between Gosford and Newcastle.

I sat at an outside table. I could see dozens of boats bobbing at their moorings among the sun-dappled water. I slid the coffee mug to one side and dabbed up the remains of the poached egg with some toasted Turkish bread. A family of four sat on the other side of the patio. They had to have been from Melbourne or maybe Tassie. They were all in shorts, t-shirts and thongs, and it wasn't even that warm yet. It was still a month away from spring, and that wind could be sharp.

But they didn't care. And between the four of them—mum, dad and a couple of porky kids—they devoured more than I could eat in a week. The table overflowed with plates, cereal bowls, pitchers of juice and cups of coffee. From the time their food arrived at their table, they had heads down like pigs at a trough. The guttural grunts even sounded like something from a barnyard. They were finishing when the little boy looked at me with a bit of that 'what you looking at me for' look on his face. About twelve or thirteen and a good candidate for Biggest

Loser - Kid's Edition.

Not that I should comment. My metabolism stopped when I was forty, and I had fourteen more years of eating takeaway wrapped around my waist.

I saluted the little tub with my cup of coffee and drained the dregs—cold and bitter. This reminded me that I still had a cheque to write. I had to drum up some business.

The family stood with ragged precision, pushing their chairs back, the metal legs scraping across the timber decking. Mom grabbed her purse, slung it over her shoulder, leaned down and wiped leftover breakfast from the boy's face. She muttered something to the daughter, who grabbed a napkin and cleaned herself off.

Dad pulled out a wallet and left some money under his coffee cup. Maybe not Australian, then. Maybe they were from overseas. Maybe South Africans. Some place that tipped.

I looked into the cafe. Jessie was at the register. Her dad owned the place. Trusted her with the money, I guess. I remember being eighteen, and if I were at the register at her age, it would be short a healthy percentage every night.

Jimmy was in there too, almost late for work, fawning over her, oblivious to her disinterest. Jimmy was a bank security guard. Jimmy was not a footy player. Jessie, therefore, would never be interested.

That didn't deter Jimmy. And I don't blame him for trying. Jessie was a very healthy, tall, sun-tanned surfer chick. If I were some thirty-five years younger, I'd be hot on that trail.

Jessie's attention was diverted from Jimmy's advances as the family of four from Melbourne or Tassie or Jo'burg walked in from the patio. The kids already had their phones out, Tweeting or whatever the hell it is they do these days. Mom must have been enforcing a 'no phones at the table' rule because now they were at them like junkies on cough syrup.

Jessie told Dad the damage, and he pulled out his wallet and offered a credit card.

I looked back at their table, trying to see what denomination he'd slid under the coffee cup. I couldn't tell. A couple of pieces of half-mauled toast and a dirty juice glass blocked my view.

The four of them ate about sixty dollars' worth

of food. Eighty, maybe, if they packed it in. A ten-dollar tip would pay for my breakfast.

Jessie finished with the family and grabbed a stack of menus, leading another family toward a larger table in the back of the place—inside, away from the patio. I left a ten under my coffee cup and strode to the tourists' table.

Dad had left a twenty. I slipped it from under the cup, folded it into my pocket without breaking stride and hopped the low fence around the patio.

"I saw that Mac, you fucking asshole."

Jessie had strong lungs.

I smiled and continued walking, waving over my shoulder. I made my escape around the corner and almost tripped over Barry.

Barry is homeless by choice. And by choice, I mean that no matter how much I, or anyone else I know, attempted to help, he still lands on his ass within staggering distance of a take-out place or a pub. It rarely got cold enough for him to worry. And when it did, he'd find a safe place to spend the night. He's a permanent reminder of our failing social services.

Smashing into Barry wasn't ideal. The grime and smell aren't permanently affixed to him, and contact spreads it. I took a quick shuffle-step to the side and nodded at him. "Baz. Nice enough out for you?"

He squinted up at me from the sidewalk. "It'll do. Anything for me?"

I grinned an apology. "Sorry, mate. I ate in this morning. Don't worry, though. Someone will have something. Don't take any wooden nickels."

"Yeah, I don't even know what that means."

I smiled and kept walking. I trotted across the street from The Pelican. A TAB advertised the final Ashes test in the window. In England this time. We had been absolutely slaughtered in the first couple of tests, and the odds for the remaining tests reflected that. A couple of NRL games were spruiked alongside in one of the windows.

It was kinda like an alcoholic having a bottle of really good scotch in his cupboard to test his resolve. My apartment-slash-office was upstairs from a place that could feed my gambling addiction forever. Well, it could feed that addiction until I ran out of money, which would be in maybe a week at the rate I was earning.

Every day I made it past the front door to the stairs up to my place was a day I won.

And I won again that morning.

The stairs to my place went up the outside of the building. They were a straight diagonal up the side wall, front to back, bottom to top—thirty-seven steps. This was usually the only exercise I got on any given day.

I ran up two at a time and stopped in front of the door. I pulled the cuff of my shirt over my hand and polished the dew off the brass plaque on the wall by the entrance. 'Mac Durridge: Private Investigator'. I gave it a final wipe and pushed open the door.

At about the same time that I registered the fact that the door was unlocked, my eyes and nose registered the fact that a long-legged blonde was sitting in the guest chair at my desk. Betty. Late-forties, daughter of the guy who owned a couple of the coal mines out of town. She was married to Ernie, an old friend from high school. Her dress cost about what I would pay for three or four months' rent. The perfume wafting from her general direction probably cost even more.

I put on my best Bogie. "There she sat, a long, tall drink of a woman, warming my seat in ways I could only dream of."

Betty spun in the chair. "Not funny, Mac. Ernie is screwing around on me, and I need you to find the slut. And get me evidence."

Just another payday.

Chapter Two

I eased the door shut and walked past her to my side of the desk. Her presence elevated the class of my place by at least an order of magnitude. Possibly more. She was one of those women who held their looks well into middle age. If anything, she looked better now than when I first met her in high school—like a blonde, strong-jawed Katherine Hepburn, crossed with Ava Gardner in her prime.

"It's always lovely to see you, Betty." I settled into my chair and calculated how much I could get from her. "So what's this about Ernie?"

She sat upright in the guest chair, probably trying

to figure out a way to levitate. Her dress no doubt resented the contact with the ten-year-old office chair. My office wasn't that flash. She held her handbag on her lap, both hands on top, mouth pursed with distaste.

"I don't like repeating myself, Mac. Ernie is screwing around on me. I need you to find out who the slut is and get me enough evidence to void the prenup. He's not getting half of my money."

"Again? You're imagining it. This is the third time, isn't it? And I haven't been able to catch him at anything. All reasonable explanations, every single time." I rifled through the centre drawer of my desk and pulled out a heavily used yellow legal pad. I rummaged a little more, extracted a pen and doodled on the top page to make sure it worked. I folded the used pages over until I came to a clean one.

"I feel bad taking your money, but I will if you insist. Ernie's as faithful as your stupid Cocker Spaniel. He would never cheat on you." I poised the pen over the pad of paper. "But tell me what you think is happening."

She narrowed her eyes and opened her purse.

Broke her gaze with me, dug through it and triumphantly pulled out a book of matches. She looked at it for a second, then threw it at me.

I grabbed it out of the air before it bounced off my face. It was from The Wayfarer, a cheap motel on the north side of town. It's one of those $59-a-night places with a very transient clientele. I held them up and looked at Betty with a question on my face.

The furrow on her brow was deep enough to plant potatoes. "I found it in a pair of his trousers. The ones he wore the night he said he had to work late."

I tapped the book of matches on my desk, then took my pen and doodled on the pad. "What did he tell you?"

"He was vague. Something about the gas system at a restaurant needing pressure testing. He wasn't back until after midnight."

I slid the matches closer. Picked the book up, balanced it on one corner and placed my index finger on the opposite corner. I slowly spun it with my other hand. I'm not Asian. I couldn't do it with one hand. Can't flip my pen over my knuckles like they do, either. "Maybe it was a restaurant near The Wayfarer. What's it called? That steak place."

She was shaking her head before I was even finished. "No, he was too clean. Like he showered."

I dropped my pen and the book of matches on the desk. "Sounds like you've got it all solved, Betty. I can't take your money." Bluffing. I would take her money in a heartbeat. And she had money to burn.

"No, I need evidence. You've got to do it."

I sighed like it was a chore. "Right. Fortunately, I've got some time on my calendar. I'll take a look at him. Mates rates, though, okay? Three hundred a day plus expenses. Shouldn't take more than a week."

She nodded, relief on her face, and reopened her purse. She pulled out an envelope, placed it on my desk and slid it toward me. "I knew you'd help. There's a thousand in here. Let me know the expenses, and I'll sort you out with the rest later." She closed her purse, prim and proper, and stood. "Thanks, Mac. Call me as soon as you know something."

She marched out. Literally marched. Head high, chest out and purse under her arm. The door closed behind her, and I listened to her shoes clacking down the stairs—thirty-seven steps down to the sidewalk.

I looked at my watch and made a mental bet with myself. Thirty seconds. Maybe thirty-five. I kept an eye on the second hand.

After twenty-three seconds, I heard someone walking up the steps. The hand swept past the thirty-one-second mark, and the door opened.

Ernie poked his head in. Where Betty was a young Kate Hepburn crossed with Ava Gardner, her husband leaned much more toward a middle-aged Peter Lorre. I couldn't figure out the attraction. Him for her, sure, but not her for him. He must be hung like a pony. "Right on schedule, Ernie. What the hell have you been up to?"

"She's gone, right? Not coming back?"

I threw the book of matches at him, and they bounced off his face and dropped to the floor. "Matches, Ernie? You don't even smoke."

He bent down and picked up the book of matches, and placed it on my desk. He settled into the chair his wife had just vacated. "For the candles?"

I leaned back. "Who?" I sat up and waved my

hands, stopping him from answering. "No, never mind. I don't want to know. I *can't* know. Why do I keep covering your ass?"

"Because you're a helluva guy?" He leaned to one side in the chair and pulled his wallet out of his back pocket. He counted off ten fifties and dropped them on my desk. "Get me out of this, Mac. Her father gets wind of this, and I'm done."

I pulled the money toward me and butted the ends, making them into a nice, neat wad of cash. "I'll do what I can, but you'll need to help me."

"Anything, man. What do you want me to do?"

I flicked the book of matches back at him. He caught it this time. "Head back there. The Wayfarer. They've got to have LPG or gas somewhere. Offer them a free inspection of their systems. Spend a *lot* of time on it. Make sure you interact with as many of the staff as you can." I stepped out from behind my desk and escorted him to the door. I held it open for him. "Be there for at least three hours. And stay away from the floozy until I've reported back to Betty."

He left, I closed the door, and I listened to him walk slowly down the stairs.

I had fifteen hundred bucks, with more coming from Betty, for what would be monkey work and a couple of pages of report that I could write this morning. I owed Ernie that much. We'd be even one of these days.

It wasn't even ten a.m., and life was looking fantastic. Then I got the phone call that started it all.

Chapter Three

I waited until Ernie was well clear of my place and walked down the stairs with a pocket full of cash. Easy money. Best kind of money. I waited for the few cars to clear and started across the street when my phone rang. I looked at the caller ID and shook my head. I swiped the screen to answer the call and plastered it to my head, keeping half an eye out for traffic. "What's up, Harris?"

Harris was the recently new manager for the local branch of a national bank. Been in town about six months, so far. Bit of a wanker, if you asked me, but he hired me on occasion if he needed an extra warm body.

"I need you at the bank ASAP, Mac. You got your gun?"

I reflexively patted under my arm and felt nothing. "Always. Why?"

"Jimmy called in sick today, and we've got a big transfer. I'm going to need some extra security."

I turned on my heel and headed back to my office for the gun. "Saw Jimmy at the cafe this morning. He looked fine to me. He was cracking hard on Jessie."

"Yeah, well, I've got a text message from him saying he's buckled himself to the dunny. I don't need or want to know anything more than that. How fast can you get here?"

The bank was down the road and on the same block as my office. "Give me ten, Harris. You're paying me, right?"

"Usual rates."

I hung up and ran up the stairs. Two sets of exercises today. Soon, I'd be as fit as Hugh Jackman. I took the revolver out of my gun safe, strapped on the shoulder holster and pulled my jacket over it.

I made it into the bank in seven minutes, a whole three minutes ahead of schedule. Sophie sat up front at one of the desks you'd go to if you were opening a new account or trying to get a loan. She smiled at me as I came in. A smile from Sophie is guaranteed to make any day, however crappy it may be, fantastic. I smiled back. I couldn't help it, really.

"Good morning, Mac. The boss is waiting for you."

"Thanks, Soph. Always great to see you." I poked my head in the first office on my left. An overweight, balding middle-aged man sat in a leather chair behind the desk. "You got something for me to sign, Harris?"

He looked up at me and pulled open the middle drawer of his desk. He pulled a single sheet out of the drawer and slid it across the desk at me. "Sign it on the bottom. And date it."

I patted my pockets. "Got a pen?"

He sighed and retrieved a nice gold pen from his inside suit pocket. I hefted it. It had a solid feel, and the ink flow was beautiful when I signed my name. I capped it, put the pen in my shirt pocket and slid the paper back across the desk.

He sat there with his hand out. "The pen, Mac."

My look of innocence lasted about three seconds. I smiled and handed it back to him. "A guy's got to try. It's a nice pen."

He stared at me for a second, then put it back in his suit pocket.

"So what do you want me to do?"

"With Jimmy out, I need another body in the back while Terry fills bags. We've got a large outgoing shipment today. Go back there and help him prep. I'll be there shortly."

I pointed at the paper on his desk. "That says I do whatever you want until six tonight."

"Tell Terry I'll be there in five. Make sure he's got all nine bags ready."

"Your wish is my command."

He grunted and pointed, and I headed toward the back. I tapped on Sophie's desk and gave her a wink. Honestly, I couldn't gauge her reaction. I *think* it was positive because why not? Other than the fact that I was a bit soft in the middle, financially, and possibly emotionally, handicapped and living out of my office—or working out of my apartment, take your pick—I was a catch, right?

The path to the door to the back room passed by a young loans officer. I hadn't seen him in the branch before. Maybe he was on a graduate program. He had a kung-fu grip on his desk phone handset and a bead of sweat on his brow. He was forcing the words down the line like caulking through a tube. "...and those terms are incredibly unfair. I told you the payment would be made—" He stopped when he saw me watching him and slowly eased the handset into the cradle.

I pointed at the door. "You got the combination to that? Harris has me working in the back with Terry."

The kid looked at Sophie. She nodded at him, and he reached over and poked a code in the keypad. He wasn't very circumspect about it. I took out my phone, entered the numbers, and saved them like phone numbers in my contacts. They might come in handy someday.

Terry looked up from the trolley he was sitting

on. He had an empty moneybag on his lap and a clipboard, filling in bag serial numbers. "Hey, Mac. You filling in for Jimmy again?"

"I think the kid's got a drinking problem. It is always on Mondays. Harris says to make sure there's nine bags ready."

"Nine bags *are* ready. Could have done it with eight."

"He said nine."

"I know, I know. When's he coming back here? We need the three of us to validate the count."

"Soon, I expect."

Terry dropped the ninth bag on the pile of eight on the trolley and stood, stretching. "So," he hesitated, "how's Jane?"

"Still a doctor-wannabe. Why. You got something for her?"

"She's your ex-wife, right? Finalised?"

"Finalised six months ago, thank God."

Terry sat back on the trolley and flipped his phone from one hand to another. Seemed kinda nervous to me. If he knew Jane like I knew Jane, he had every right to be nervous. "Don't let me get in the way, Terry. Just don't complain to me when she busts your balls. And by bust, I mean crush them and sprinkle the crumbs on a banana split."

"How long were you married?"

Small talk makes me want to pluck out my eyes. Or someone else's. "Too long. When's the truck showing up?"

"A couple of hours. It'll take us that long to validate the count." He cleared his throat. "So, you never told me why you broke up?"

I squinted in his general direction, slipped my phone into my pocket and hung my jacket on the end of the trolley. "You're right. I didn't." I checked the time. "It takes two hours?"

"If we rush. It's a lot this time."

Harris pushed through the door, his shirtsleeves rolled up to his elbows. "Okay, boys. Let's get this done."

Chapter Four

We spent all of those two hours on the most boring, repetitive—look, if you had told me that being surrounded by four-and-a-half million in cash would have me longing for the excitement of drying paint and growing grass, I would have laughed you out of town.

Harris would count a stack, handed it to Terry, who counted the same stack and then Terry handed it to me to count. By 'count,' I mean stick the wad of bills in a money counting machine, a different one for each of us, and read the number off the display. It seemed very strange to me, but what the hell? I was getting paid for it.

If all three counts are identical, then the wad of cash was wrapped. If the count wasn't the same for all three, the process was repeated for all three of us. That happens more often than you'd think.

We ended up with nine moneybags filled and locked, half a mill each.

The bags had a serial number—six digits printed in large block numbers on the body of the bag.

I loaded each bag onto the trolley, and Terry read the bag's serial number and wrote it on a form on a clipboard.

I hoisted the fourth bag on the trolley and reached for the fifth when Terry held out his hand to stop me.

"Harris, are the last two digits on this one 'one-seven' or 'seven-seven'?" Terry held the pen poised over the clipboard.

Harris squatted down and pulled the bag closer. "That's a 'seven-seven'. I'll fix it." He creaked upright and grabbed a felt-tipped marker off a table. He filled in the missing top part of the first 'seven', his tongue stuck firmly between his lips. He held the bag at a slight distance and squinted. "Perfect." He pushed the bag back onto the trolley and capped the marker. "Keep it going, lads. The truck will be here any minute."

I lugged the last five bags onto the trolley. Terry logged the serial numbers and handed the list to Harris.

Harris handed it back without looking at it. "Sign it first."

Terry scrawled across the bottom, shaking his head, and handed it back. "Okay?"

The bank manager smiled and scanned the list quickly, countersigned it and placed it on top of the bags of cash. "Mac, you sit tight with these until the truck gets here. It'll be about fifteen minutes."

I looked at the stack of bags on the trolley. "That's a hell of a lot of money, Harris. You trust me?"

"Shouldn't I?" He pulled his suit jacket off the back of the chair. "Most secure room in the place." He waved generically at the ceiling. "Cameras every-fucking-where. I don't need to trust you. You're here to satisfy insurance regulations."

The prick. I took out my phone and snapped pictures of the pile of money bags. It really was more money than I'd ever seen before. I snapped a couple of extras: the room, lanky Terry, and a few with the flash on in Harris' face to piss him off.

"Fuck off with the camera," said Harris. "I'm grabbing a coffee. You want one?"

"Black, thanks."

I was halfway through a large long black when Harris pushed into the room.

"Mac, head to the back. The truck's here. Hold the door. I'll be behind you with the trolley. Terry, go with him. Make sure the route is secure."

The 'route' was a bendy hallway no longer than thirty or forty metres. I went through the back door out of the room and, after about ten steps, hit a T-intersection. "Left or right, Harris?" I looked back over my shoulder. "Which way?"

Harris looked up from the clipboard. "Wazzat? Go right."

So I went right, and then the hallway angled left and dead in front of me was the door to the loading area. I pushed it open just as the armoured truck rolled to a stop. Its tail lined up with the door. Two armed guards jumped out, one standing with his hand on his sidearm beside the truck and the other walking to the back.

He looked up and nodded at me. "You with the bank?"

"Yeah. Money will be here in a minute."

The guard beside the truck continued a conversation they had obviously been having in the truck. "I don't fucking believe it. Son of a bitch."

I nodded toward the stationary guard and looked at the one closer to me. "What the hell's he on about?"

"Three of the NSW squad have been done for doping. Banned from playing for club or Origin side until the investigation's complete."

"Seriously? That's fantastic." I smiled at him. He didn't look like he was enjoying my pleasure.

"Are you fucking nuts?"

"I've got a tonne on Queensland." I didn't, really. Gambling problem, right? I just liked winding these hardcores up. "So, you guys ready?"

Terry pushed the door open. "You guys ready?"

"I just asked that, Terry. We need to coordinate a bit more. Where's the cash?"

"Harris is triple-checking the serial numbers." He looked back into the bank. "Here he is. Grab the door, Mac." He ducked back into the bank and, a second later, backed out with the trolley. Harris walked out after him with the clipboard.

The guard doing the hard work opened the truck door and took the clipboard from Harris. He scanned through the nine serial numbers, placed the clipboard on the cargo area floor and started moving the bags. As each one was placed in the truck, he initialled beside the corresponding serial number on the log.

When all nine were loaded, the guard signed the bottom of the sheet and returned the list to Harris. He countersigned and nodded at the guard. "Good to go, son."

I watched the guard lock the cargo area, and as both guards were entering the truck, I let out a yell. "Go, the Maroons!" I think they heard me.

"You're a bit of a prick, you know that?"

I looked at Harris. "So that's it, then? Can you

pay me in cash?"

"Trying to stiff the tax man? Sophie will cut you a cheque. Like always."

"You give me a cheque and half of it goes to my fucking ex."

Harris smiled as he held the door to the back of the bank for me. "Not my problem. Sophie will cut you a cheque."

Chapter Five

I stopped by Sophie's desk on the way out of the bank and perched myself on the corner of her desk. I looked at her, saying nothing, just smiling.

She glanced at me, then back to whatever was on her monitor that was taking her attention.

I waited. It wasn't a chore. Sophie's jet-black hair was pulled back in a ponytail, and her large-framed glasses were half-slid down her nose. The muscles in her arms, the small muscles, moved in time with whatever she was typing. I am a lousy judge of genetic makeup, but if I had to guess which part of the Mediterranean her forefathers hailed from, I'd be putting money on either Egypt or maybe Syria. Maybe Lebanon. Like I said, I'm a lousy judge. But a dusky, almond-eyed beauty either way. Slim, trim, and very fit. I'm not even going to say 'fit for her age'. She was only a few years younger than me, and she was fit for someone half her age.

She finally gave up waiting for me to say something. "What, Mac? You're on my desk."

"Harris said you'd be cutting me a cheque, although if it's not a problem, I'd prefer cash."

She continued typing. "Harris will send the paperwork to me by email sometime today. I'll add it to my pile of stuff to do, and in the next day or so, a cheque will be posted to the address we have for you." She stopped typing and looked up at me, a small smile on her face. "Just like we always do."

I used both hands to push myself off the corner of the desk and shook out my trouser legs. "Perfect. It has been a delight talking to you, Soph. We should do it more often."

I saluted her with two fingers and walked out into the warm sunshine. I stood at the front door and looked across the street at Barry sitting against the cafe wall, half asleep. I looked left, up the road at my apartment-slash-office, back at Barry, and crossed the street. I popped into the cafe, grabbed a couple of coffees and came back out, sitting on the sidewalk beside Barry.

I handed him one of the cups. "What's new, Baz?"

He took the cup and nodded at me slightly, and lifted it to his lips. He took a sip, then screwed up his face and made like he was handing the coffee back to me. "Too much sugar."

I looked at the cup and then back at Barry. "Really?" I reached for it, and he pulled it back and took another sip.

"It'll do in a pinch, I guess." A stream of coffee etched its way through the stubble on his chin and added to the kaleidoscope of crap on his shirt. "Catch any bad guys lately?"

"Slow as shit, Baz. What you been up to?"

He grinned his yellowed teeth at me. "The usual. Taking care of my investments and planning the next trip to my villa in Monaco." He pointed to my hand. "You're flashing."

I looked where he was pointing. My phone was still on silent, and Harris's number was flashing on my screen. I patted Barry on the shoulder and stood. "What's up, Harris? You want to hire me again?"

"Get your ass back here, right now. We got a serious fucking problem."

Harris, your friendly neighbourhood banker, hard at work.

Harris walked Terry and me into the same backroom I'd spent two hours counting money in and locked the door behind us.

Terry's Adam's apple bobbed like it was actively working on an escape. "What's going on, boss?"

I folded my arms across my chest and leaned back against the wall. Harris unbuttoned his sleeves and rolled them up, put his hands on his hips and started pacing the small room. He opened his mouth three or four times to start a sentence, then shook his head and kept pacing. When he finally stopped to talk, his face was a bright red, and a bead of sweat lined his upper lip.

"We were all here for the count today. No breaks

in security the entire time, right? We all saw the money go in the bags, the bags on the trolley, and then off the trolley and into the truck, right?"

Terry nodded. "Counted three times. Double-checked the serial numbers. You triple-checked them."

I stayed against the wall, my mouth shut. This didn't look good.

Harris nodded and took a step toward Terry. "Exactly. Triple-checked the serial numbers on the bags." He turned, standing beside Terry, and looked at me, making it feel very much like a two-against-one situation. "Is that how you remembered it, Mac?"

I uncrossed my arms and pushed off the wall. "What in the hell is going on here? Harris, you look like someone just told you you've got ball cancer."

"I'd rather that, believe me." He wiped moisture from the corners of his mouth. "We're all clear that the bags went into the truck without being opened after we filled them, right?"

I nodded. Terry did the same. Harris wiped the sweat off his brow with his shirt sleeve. "Good. Excellent. It has to have been the guys on the truck then. I'll make sure there's a full enquiry. I'll send a copy of the surveillance video from in here."

This was going on too long. "Right. So what in the hell happened?"

"The bags. When they got to the destination, they were all filled with cut-up paper. Newspapers, magazines, jam-packed, and not a single piece of currency."

Terry leaned over, his eyes huge. "No way. That was four and a half mill. It's gone?"

Harris unlocked the door and held his hand on the knob. "Details stay in this room, okay? I've got to call the police." He opened the door. "In my office."

We followed him through the branch to his office. Sophie caught my eye and furrowed her brow like she was asking a question. I shrugged and mouthed 'later'. She glanced quickly at Harris and then back at me and nodded.

Harris' office looked like the kind of office you'd expect a senior player in the financial sector to have. Except, he was only the manager of a tiny branch of a massive national bank. Way down the pecking order. A massive mahogany desk populated the far side of the office, with a floor-to-ceiling window behind him. Two leather chairs sat in front of the desk for visitors, and a leather sofa stretched along the near wall. Whiskey bottles lined shelves on the wall on the left, and a small bar fridge sat below another handsome table—an office fit for a king.

He pointed at the two chairs as he made his way around the desk. "Sit."

I ignored his direction and stretched my legs out on the sofa. It was very comfortable. He looked at me momentarily, shook his head and made a call.

I didn't pay much attention to what he was saying. Framed pictures covered the wall above the sofa. You couldn't see them if you just popped a head in the office, but from his vantage point at his desk, they constantly reminded him of how cool he was. Photos with John Howard and Johnny Depp, signed. Chris Hemsworth, signed. Numerous other Australian celebrities, all signed. The guy thought a lot of himself by proxy.

He dropped the phone in the cradle and tapped on his desk to get my attention. "The cops are on their way. We need to give them a statement."

"Who were you talking to?" I know most of them. Some I get along well with, and others I'd shoot if given half the chance.

"Thomas."

"Superintendent Thomas, to you." I nodded. "Good guy. He's not coming, though. Who's he sending?"

"Who cares?" Harris wiped the back of his neck. "I think he was calling for King as he hung up."

Lily King was good. Barely over the height requirement, barely under the weight requirement, and sharp as a tack. Detective (Sergeant) King. One of the better ones. I looked at my watch and shrugged. "No skin off my back. You're still paying me. And if it goes past 6:00, it's extra."

"What-ever-the-fuck, Mac."

Terry leaned back in his chair and dry-scrubbed his face, then ran his fingers through his thinning hair. "This is a mess."

Harris leaned forward. "Hey, we're in the clear. Three of us were present when we filled the bags. We logged the bag numbers and the armoured car guys signed off on them. We are absolutely in the clear.

Security cameras will confirm it."

I laced my fingers behind my head and rested on the sofa arm, my legs stretched out the length of the sofa. I closed my eyes and smiled. "It's never that easy, Harris, and you know it. I'll give my statement to the cops, but there's something else going on here. I can feel it."

"So you're volunteering to investigate this for me?"

I laughed at Harris. "Hell no, man. I've got some pressing work I've got to do for Betty." I wasn't going to touch this with a barge pole.

Sophie stuck her head in the office. "The police are here." She stood to one side, and Tom Jackson oozed in.

I swung my feet to the floor and stood. "You're not Lily." He was one of the ones I'd gladly shoot.

"You're not wrong. Why am I not surprised that you're here, Mac?" He pulled out a pad and fished a pencil from his shirt pocket. "Okay, I understand there's been a robbery. How much did they get, and what did they look like?"

I sat back on the sofa, crossed my legs and

folded my arms. A not-so-subliminal body language message of 'fuck you'. "This should be interesting. One of the more audacious and clever robberies I've ever heard of, being investigated by a guy who most definitely isn't smarter than a fifth grader. How are your wife and my kid, Jackson? How *is* little Davey? Does he look anything like me yet?"

Jackson pointed at me and looked at Harris. "Does he need to be here?" He looked at me. "Do you need to be here? Why are you here?"

"By all means, let me leave. But if you had half a brain in that pumpkin, you'd get a statement from me before you completely fuck it up."

"I'll do you last."

I laced my fingers behind my head and leaned back. "Excellent."

Chapter Six

Jackson was a lot more thorough than he needed to be. At least with Harris and Terry. I'm pretty sure that was to keep me there as long as possible. I didn't care. Harris was paying for my time, and if I was there, Jackson was there, and I knew for a fact that I was making more than he was.

He went around the circle half a dozen times, walked the path from the counting room to the loading bay twice, looked at the video at 6x speed and then took a copy of it, and then talked to me. He got nothing new from our conversation.

He was about to start in on Terry again when

Harris placed a hand on his arm. "Jackson, there's nothing we haven't told you. If anything else comes up, we'll contact you. Is that okay? The horse is dead. It's time to stop flogging it."

Jackson looked at the three of us for a second, then closed the notepad, looked at his watch and smiled. "Damn. Almost eight. I'll let you guys get back to your lives."

I pushed past him, a slightly harder nudge than really necessary and stood at the locked bank door. "Come on, Harris. Open up. And make sure my hours include this, right?"

I stepped into the chill evening air with Terry and Jackson. Harris still had paperwork to do. Not a job I'd ever want. The Pelican blared 'Wanted: Dead or Alive' at a slightly faster tempo than the original, but it wasn't bad. A burger and a beer would go down well.

Jackson's a dick.

I hadn't even taken the step off the curb to cross the road when he jumped in front of me, jabbing his porky finger in my sternum. I looked down at the digit, then into his piggy eyes. "You want to fuck off, mate, before I shove that finger where you usually keep it."

"You're a suspect in this."

"And so are Terry and Harris. So fucking what?" I pushed him away. "Video clears us. You saw it. Go do some real detecting, fuckrag. I'm hungry. Outta my way." I gave him a shove again. It was a little harder than necessary and as I stepped off the curb I forgot about him almost immediately.

It was warm inside The Pelican. The combined heat of dozens of sweaty, dancing, horny people. I leaned on the bar and caught Jessie's attention. Her eyes narrowed when she saw me, but she came over anyway.

"What do you want?"

I slipped a fifty out of my pocket. One of Ernie's. "Cheeseburger with the works and a beer. Keep the change." I winked at her. She seemed mollified somewhat. She got her twenty-dollar tip back. Plus some. "I'll be over in the corner."

She pulled the schooner of beer, and I took it with me, shouldering my way through the crowd to a corner table.

The bank thing was confusing. Between Terry, Harris and myself, the money was covered the entire time. But the two guys in the truck didn't seem to have enough smarts to set the time on a microwave. I shook my head. Fuck it. I wasn't investigating it. Fuckrag Jackson was. The list of people I would willingly run over with a bus was short, but he was at the top.

A server pushed her way through the crowd and deposited a double burger with chips in front of me. "Jessie says thanks."

I nodded and dipped a chip into the small bowl of tomato sauce. Just my luck, Jackson pulled this case, and not Lily. Lily King was competent. Jackson was an idiot. Like the armoured car crew, not much good for anything. If Lily were on the case, I'd feel comfortable that it might eventually get cleared. Jackson, on the other hand, was going to blunder through whatever excuse he could come up with, and this would either go cold or, worse, he'd peg the wrong guy. And given our history, I had a pretty good idea of who that wrong guy would be.

The burger was good, and the chips were salted

just right. I was on her good side again. I belched and stretched. I'm pretty sure it's common, but I've noticed that the older I got, the higher sleep moved up my list of desirable things to do. And clubbing slid down the list. Fuck. Pretty soon, I'd be chasing kids off my front lawn. If I had a front lawn.

I tipped back the glass, drained the dregs of the beer and pushed my way out of the club. Copped a couple of gropes on the way. Not as exciting as it used to be.

The night was crisper now. Although it was still dropping to single digits, the sky was perfectly clear. I looked up at the millions of stars and took a deep breath, exhaling a thick cloud of warm air.

Back across the road and half a block up from the bank to the TAB and my daily exercise. I ran up the stairs two at a time and stopped short of pushing open my door.

It was already open, just wide enough to get a hand in.

I removed my handgun from its holster and slowly opened the door with my left hand. "I'm armed, and you're an idiot if you're sitting in the dark waiting for me." I listened hard. 'Living on a Prayer' seeped out from across the street. A dog barked a couple of blocks away. A throaty muffler barked as a car started somewhere in the neighbourhood. But nothing from inside.

I felt along the inside wall until I hit the light switch. Nothing looked disturbed. The door to my room in the back was open, though, and I'm almost certain I had closed it when I left earlier. I slowly pushed that door open a little wider and looked in. Nothing. The bed was still a mess. Half a beer on the side table. Nobody had broken in and cleaned up.

I put my gun and holster in the gun safe and closed and locked the front door. There really wasn't anything of any value in here. The computer on the desk was almost ten years old and took a week to start up. I only used it to write reports, and I'm pretty sure I could do just as well with a typewriter. No, there was nothing of any real value at all.

Except for the files, I guess. I checked the file cabinets. There were three of them on the wall opposite my desk. I didn't do a complete inventory, but a casual glance through all the drawers didn't show anything obviously missing. No gaps. There are no out-of-sequence tabs in the file folders.

I must have left the door open when I left.

Except I don't usually do that.

I sat at my desk and checked the drawers. They never contained anything more than stationary supplies, and they didn't seem to have been disturbed.

Weird.

It was too late to worry much more about it. I couldn't call the police for a break-in when nothing appeared to have been taken.

I yawned. A problem for another day.

Chapter Seven

I pushed the covers off and swung my feet onto the floor. I leaned forward and held my head in my hands. "Tuesday? Tuesday. What am I supposed to be doing today? I need a—" I stopped myself. "I need coffee."

A shave, shit and a shower later, and I was walking across the street to the cafe. Someone else worked the till and served me my bag of pastries and two coffees. It was like a wake in there. Jessie was in a corner booth, crying and getting consoled by her mother, the other staff and customers in a sombre mood.

I left and sat down beside Barry and handed him a coffee and a bag of pastries. I took the bag, extracted a cinnamon doughnut and handed it back.

"What the hell is going on in there, Baz? Somebody die?"

Barry gently placed the coffee on the sidewalk between his feet and peered into the brown bag.

"Ya got it in one, Mac. Young Jimmy. Jessie's shattered."

"Shit." I looked over my shoulder into the cafe. "Didn't think she liked him that much."

He pulled out a bear claw and smelled it. "Women. Go figure." He took a dainty bite from the end, determined it was satisfactory and jammed the rest of it into his gaping maw.

I watched with a twinge of revulsion. "Eternal mysteries, women. What happened to Jimmy?"

"Beat to death, I heard. Down at the beach."

"Ah, he deserved better than that. Cops pick anyone up?"

Barry shook his head. "No suspects, I heard."

This was a twist on an already ugly situation.

"What you thinking about, Mac?"

"It's going to get pretty smelly around here."

"You talking about me?"

I looked over at Barry and smiled. "No more than usual. No, I mean we've got a weird-assed bank robbery, and the next day, the bank guard is beaten to death."

"He was beaten to death yesterday. They just found him today."

"Yeah, that's not a coincidence." I leaned back against the wall and looked across the street. I had a clear view up the stairs to my office. Perfect angle. I nudged Barry. "Hey, Baz, you see anyone go into my place last night?"

He laughed, spilling coffee down the front of his shirt. "Last night? An elephant could have marched past and shit on my shoes, and I wouldn't have noticed." He wiped coffee out of his beard. "You had visitors?"

"Maybe."

"You call the cops?"

It was my turn to laugh. "I'm a fucking detective, Baz. I'll figure it out myself." I looked at him again. He was getting pretty rank. "I'm going beach fishing this arvo. You want to come along?"

He nodded while he drank coffee, more spilling through his beard and onto his shirt. "Sounds like a plan. You know where to find me."

I smacked him on the shoulder and stood. "That I do. I've got bills to pay, Baz, but you wouldn't know anything about that."

He smiled up at me and gave me the thumbs up.

The Wayfarer was one of those places you drive by and wonder who in the hell would stay there. It was all rustic timber, small cabins spread out in concentric arcs from the main office. The 'Vacancy' sign was always lit. The 'No' was never lit. I couldn't remember seeing more than three or four cars there, ever. Its business plan just had to include some money laundering, or it would have folded years ago.

I parked my shit-box Corolla at the front door and walked into an empty lobby. I knocked on the counter a couple of times. "Hello. Anybody home?"

A door behind the receptionist counter opened, and a pimply-faced kid stuck his head out. "Can I help you?"

I nodded him over and opened a photo on my phone. Ernie, face on. I held it up and tapped it with my finger. "You ever see this guy before? Was he checking your gas fittings out recently?"

The kid took the phone and squinted at the picture, tongue out, deep in thought. "Yeah, yeah. I know this guy."

"Checking your gas, right?"

"That, yeah." He snapped his fingers. "And he was here a couple of days ago with—"

"Don't need to know about that," I interrupted. "Just the gas."

"Yeah, but—"

"No 'yeah-buts'. Not even a bunny yeah-but. Thanks for the info." I took the phone back and got the hell out of there before he compromised my investigation with facts. I scrolled through my phone and called Ernie, putting it on speaker and lodging it in the phone holder stuck to my dash.

"That you, Mac?"

I started the car. "Where you at?"

"Burger place out by the highway. They got a new system installed. Need an independent audit for insurance. Why?"

I yanked the car around in a U-turn, enveloped in a cloud of my own smoke. "Gonna pop by and take a few pictures for the report. I was just at the Wayfarer. You've got to be a hell of a lot more discrete, mate."

Chapter Eight

It was mid-afternoon before I got back to Baz. Ernie had probably one of the most boring jobs in the world until it wasn't. Meticulously testing gas joints for leaks, with nothing to show for it until something blew up, then all hell would break loose.

No hell broke loose this afternoon.

I pulled up in front of the café, leaned over and pushed the passenger side door open. I tapped the horn. "Baz, you fucking lump, get your ass in the car."

He was reclined on the sidewalk, enjoying his daily siesta. I tapped the horn again.

"Fuck off!" Other than his mouth, nothing moved.

"Fishing, Baz. Come on." It was a community service I was trying to do. Honest. I tapped the horn again.

He opened one eye and glared at me as much as one can glare from a reclined position. He groaned and pushed himself to a sitting position. "Asshole."

"I thought you wanted to go fishing."

"I was sleeping. Dreaming about that Scarlett girl. Youse got no fucking manners."

"Get in, Baz. You'll thank me later."

He stretched and looked around at his surroundings. "Take my stuff with me?"

"Why not? Put some hustle in it, Baz. Time and tide wait for no man. Especially tide. Get a hump on. I want some yellowtail. Hurry your ass. We'll grill them on the beach after we catch them."

Barry collected his few belongings and stowed them in a cheap nylon duffle. He leaned in the car and tossed the bag in the back seat, just missing two fishing poles and a small round barbecue.

He slid into the passenger seat. "Won't get any

yellowtail today."

"Think positive, Baz."

"I am positive. You're not that smart. It's July. No yellowtail. Groper, maybe."

I looked at him as he pulled the door shut. "Wind down your window, mate." I did the same for mine. "It's August. Has been for a couple of weeks. But I take your point. Not likely we'll find any yellowtail."

We drove in silence for a few minutes. I adjusted my window, trying to set it up so the wind blew from my side to his. The stench was powerful. I finally gave up. I'd have to burn the car, I guess.

I changed the subject to get the smell off my mind. "I've been thinking about Jimmy."

"Huh?"

"He called in sick Monday. Harris called me to cover for him."

"So you were there on Monday? How in the fuck does a bank lose over four million bucks?"

"Ha. I wish I knew. Harris wanted me to investigate it, but that's a mug's game. Let the cops handle that one." I chuckled. "But if the best they have working on it is Jackson, it's going to go cold."

Barry looked at me. "Ask yourself why him, maybe." I swerved to avoid a fuck-knuckle on a bike, slamming Barry against the door. "Okay, or not."

I shrugged. "Luck of the draw, I expect. So what happened to Jimmy? He was hassling Jessie Monday morning. Didn't look sick to me. Lovesick, maybe."

Barry snugged his seatbelt. "Cops think it was a mugging, I guess." He looked over at me. "You don't, though. Do you?"

I changed lanes and pulled into the beach parking lot and turned off the car. "It doesn't explain why he called in sick." I grabbed the rods and barbeque from the back seat. "Hey, Baz, what you say you go for a swim and wash off some of that stink while I set things up?" I told you. Public service.

"Good idea, mate." He turned to the water and walked until he was waist-deep, then dove in. Pants, shirt, boots, jacket and all. That wasn't exactly what I had in mind.

I set the barbecue up on the sand and lit the charcoals. It would take a good hour to get a nice bed of red coals. I stuck some bait on the hooks, threw them out, planted both poles in the sand and waited. I sat on the sand and watched Barry. He was concerning some of the parents with kids, but other than the smell, he was harmless.

I was just relaxing into the afternoon sun when I had tugs on both lines simultaneously. "Baz, get your arse over here and help."

He staggered to shore, and I handed him a rod. "Bring it in. It's yours." I wrestled my fish to shore and cleaned it. Barry fought his with more energy than I'd seen him expend in months. I helped him pull it in and clean it. I ground some salt and pepper on both of them and dropped them on the grill.

Barry shuffled closer to the heat, seawater dripping from his beard and jacket. "Brilliant fucking idea, going for a swim."

"Hey, mate, I didn't tell you to go in with your clothes on." I laughed at him, though. He was shivering like a Chihuahua shitting razor blades. "Get near the heat before you catch pneumonia."

He moved closer, water dripping and sizzling on the charcoals.

"I think that's a bit too close. You put out that

fire, we're having sushi for dinner. Back it off half a step."

He complied. "So why do you do this for me, Mac? Most people I know pretty much ignore me. Which, if I'm honest, is fine with me. It's better than the ones who kick me or spit on me."

"We're most of us just one paycheque away from being in the same boat as you. Figure I may as well make a friend or two on your side of the street before I end up there myself." I flipped the fish. "You're a relatively smart guy. I've met dumber. Hell, my current client is dumber. Both of them. Why are you on the street?"

Barry spread his arms out in a cross-shape. "I gots everything I need right here. That fish ready? I'm starving."

"Almost. You may as well take that coat off and dry your shirt, anyway. That coat's going to take forever."

Chapter Nine

I dropped Barry back at the cafe, his hangout of choice. He'd eaten most of the fish, which was fine by me. Not a huge Groper fan. I really would have preferred Yellowtail, in season or not. I was a little concerned that his jacket was still wet and it was getting dark, but he assured me that he had it sorted, that it wasn't his first rodeo and half a dozen other clichés.

I parked behind my building and scaled the stairs a little slower than usual. A day at the beach can really wear you out. Even if it is only a half-day at the beach.

I unlocked the door—no sign of intruders this time—and stepped into the darkness. A white rectangle on the floor caught my attention—an envelope. I must be getting paranoid. My first thought was 'arsenic', and I quickly changed that thought to 'anthrax' because that's what I meant the first time. Come on, give me a break. I was tired.

I picked it up carefully by the edges, though if it *was* deadly, it was extremely unlikely the perpetrator would leave prints. People just aren't that dumb anymore. I gave it a light shake. It didn't feel like there was loose powder in there. I opened a penknife, carefully cut along the top edge and buckled the side to open the envelope like a pocket. It was a cheque with a piece of notepaper folded around it.

The cheque was made out to me, personally, not my business, and in the amount of $1,000. Around four hundred more than I was expecting. I read the note:

Thanks for filling in on short notice. This should make up for the long night. Harris.

Huh. The guy's not as big a jerk as I thought he was. "Day's not turning out that bad." I folded the cheque, stuck it in my wallet and sat at my desk. I had a report to prepare for Betty. Strictly speaking, the 'investigation' wouldn't be complete until Saturday, but it was a foregone conclusion, right? I may as well get the report out of the way now.

I typed up a 'verbatim' interview with the pimply Wayfarer manager, confirming that Ernie was there for gas-related issues, then added some photos from the burger place job. I plugged in a few more 'observations' from days yet to occur, and it was ready to go. I dated the report for the following Sunday, saved it, and sent it to the printer across the room.

I had it in my hand, heading back to my desk when my door smashed open, and Jackson barged in, gun in one hand, folded piece of paper in the other and two uniforms behind him.

I dropped the report on the desk and got in front of Jackson. "This is getting ridiculous. Doesn't anybody knock anymore?"

Jackson unfolded the paper and waved it in my face. I noted that he still held his sidearm in his hand. He leaned forward. "I've got a warrant for your arrest and to search your premises."

I kept an eye on his handgun. "What the fuck? What's the warrant for, banging your old lady?" The gun hand rose a couple of centimetres, and I stepped back and held my hands up. "Just kidding, mate. What's this about?"

"Ya robbed the bank, hot shot. Surprised you hung around with that kind of money in your pocket."

Wow. That was like a gut punch. I sat down in my chair and waved around the office. "You're really off base with this one. Go ahead. Search. There's nothing in here. And Harris will vouch for me. I didn't rob any bank."

"Not my problem, asshole. You got a good lawyer? Hope not." He pulled handcuffs from the holder on the back of his belt. "Put these on." He looked over his shoulders at the uniforms. "Search this place like you're a stoner, and there's Doritos in here."

"None of that either, Jackhole. I'm not leaving until the search is complete. I don't trust you."

Jackson stood over me, sour sweat fouling my nose. "Put on the cuffs, or I'll put them on you myself."

I stood and pushed him. "Put 'em away. I'll go."

Jackson stood too close, inside my personal space, and he wasn't paying rent in my personal space, so I gave him a hard shove and turned to pick up my phone from the desk. The little fuck sucker punched me, catching me in the kidney. I fell forward onto the desk and knocked my phone onto the floor. I winced as I bent down to pick it up. "That hurt. You'll pay for that."

"Threatening a cop. I'll add that to the list."

I so badly wanted to smash the smug smile off Jackson's face, but there'd be time for that later. I'd make sure of it.

I took the cuffs from his hand and put them on. Jackson led me out as the two uniforms went through my file drawers. "I swear to God, you two, if anything's missing when all this is done, I'm suing you and the department—you both, personally. I'm going to need a full inventory."

I doubt they heard the last parts of that. Jackson was shoving me down the stairs, and it was all I could do to keep my balance.

Chapter Ten

Well, that was fun. I've processed plenty of perps, but this was the first time I sat on that side of the table. Yeah, maybe I was a bit of a dick about cooperating, but fuck Jackson and the horse he came in on.

The night in jail was, fortunately, in isolation. I may not be a cop, but I was one in the not-that-distant past, and there were a few boys who wouldn't mind beating my skull against a concrete wall. It wasn't like it was solitary—they kept me in a holding cell. Jackson popped by every twenty minutes or so, trying to get a rise from me. I didn't bite. I'm not an idiot.

They didn't feed me breakfast. Something about not having enough time to get it and get back to me before the bail hearing, but that was bullshit, too. I was taken from the cell to an ante-room and sat there for three hours before the hearing. And the hearing was the worst part of the entire experience. Not because of the judge. I knew him from my time on the force. He was pretty lenient. The horrible part was who posted bail.

I walked out of the courthouse with my ex-wife, Jane. We stopped at the top step. I looked at her and debated a kiss on the cheek and decided it wasn't worth the potential kick in the nuts. "Thanks for bailing me out."

"Add it to the next cheque. Which is due if my dates are correct."

"Right." I looked for her car. "Lincoln here?"

"Why would I have him with me? I came here from work, and I've got to get back to work."

"Just because a judge gave you custody doesn't make him yours. He's mine."

"I think the fact a judge made that decree means precisely that I'm Lincoln's owner. Suck it. I really need to go."

"The oldest intern in Australia."

Jane crossed her arms. "I'm finally doing what I want to do. Splitting with you was the best thing I've ever done."

"When are you going to get married and put me out of this financial misery?"

She flipped me the bird, got into her ancient Holden and left without even looking back.

"You're better off without her, mate." A hand clapped me on the shoulder. A big, fat meaty hand. It was accompanied by a wave of cheap cologne.

I closed my eyes, sighed and turned and looked at my solicitor, Alfred Dean. "Alfie, she's got my dog. I don't care about her. I want my dog back. Get my dog back, Alfie."

"You've got larger problems, my son."

I wiped the corners of my mouth. I was beginning to froth. "This is a gee up. There's no way they've got evidence implicating me in any robbery. In fact, Alf, there's evidence that clears me. Get the video from the bank. From the back room. There's a video of me when I was allegedly robbing the bank, in the presence of two of the bank's officers in a secure room. I watched it with Jackson, Harris and Terry. I know it exists. Get a fucking copy, okay?"

"I'm trying to get that. Discovery will be in a couple of days."

"Don't wait for that. Get the video and kill this off."

Alf had a look of concern I hadn't seen on his ruddy face in years.

"You look like you just ran over a puppy, Alf. What's wrong?"

"The cops have something. You saw Jackson."

I started walking down the stairs. "He's always like that."

Alf walked beside me, shaking his head. "A different level of malicious glee. Keep an eye out. Watch your back. He's got something up his sleeve."

My stomach growled. "Let me worry about him. You get the video from the bank and shut this down. Call me when you get something, okay? I need to get some food."

Chapter Eleven

There was a crowd at Jessie's place, and I really didn't feel like a crowd right now. Nazmi Tabeesh ran a decent kebab shop right next door, and it was the kind of food that felt right. And Nazmi was a friend. Seven years ago, when he was fifteen, I busted him stealing cars. I knew he wasn't one of the usual crowd in Gosford, and he was scared shitless. Not at all like the rest of the mob he was hanging with. During interviews, it came out that his old man was already in for drugs, and he was a loose cannon. I had a come-to-Jesus talk with him—not really Jesus, given his Muslim upbringing—and I think I got through. I put in a good word for him and kept his sentence low and in juvie. I put him in touch with a friend and got him off the streets. From his point of view, I was a do-gooder who couldn't keep his nose out of other people's business. From my point of view, Nazmi was a 1.9m, 100-kilo friend, and I didn't want to have to run up against him when he got really jacked. My friend took him under his wing, and within five years, Nazmi was running the shop and doing a damned good job.

I pushed the door open, and the bell above the door tinkled. Nazmi was slicing meat off the stack of chicken slowly turning on the vertical spit. He turned when I walked in.

"Mac, what the fuck. Arrested? You?"

"I was framed, your honour. Get me a meat lover's pide, no cheese. Extra jalapeño."

'You got it. Ten minutes.' He started putting the dish together. "What were you arrested for?"

"You probably heard more than I did, mate." I nodded at the onions. "Don't forget those."

"The bank thing? No way."

"That's what they say." I leaned against the

counter and looked up at the ceiling. There was a security camera in the corner, facing the till. "That thing hooked up?"

"Yeah. And one at the door to catch people coming in and out."

I opened the door and looked up at the inverted dome above the door. Across the street from my office.

I came back in as Nazmi was putting the jalapeños on. "More. You know better than that." I jacked my thumb toward the door. "I need to see the footage from that one, from a couple of nights ago. I had a visitor."

Nazmi slid the tray with my lunch into the small oven. "Come on back." He led me into the back room. "You're a fuckin' PI, man. Shouldn't you have your own security system?"

"I'm beginning to think that."

Nazmi woke up a computer screen and opened a video file dated two days earlier. "Scroll through this. I need to get back up front."

I waited for him to leave, then pressed the spacebar to start the video. A digital clock was superimposed on the lower right-hand corner. I used the mouse to scrub forward to four in the afternoon, then played it at 6X speed. At 5:43, a black truck stopped in front of the TAB, and two guys got out. The resolution that far away was too poor to identify anyone, but they were big lads. One turned to someone off-screen, said something, and then laughed.

"Who or what are you laughing at?"

They ascended the stairs to my office, tried the door and walked in. "Fuck. I've really got to remember to lock the door." A couple of minutes later, they both walked out, got back in the truck, and drove away.

I rewound the video and watched it again. A bog-standard black ute, and faces that are just brownish-pink blobs with no features. One of them, the driver, had a shaved head, but that's half the male population over forty these days. Everybody wants to be Bruce Willis. The other had shaggy hair, but again, that's the other half of the population.

I played it again and paused it when they were a few steps up the stairs. The bald one had something white sticking out of his back pocket. I scrubbed forward until the driver was getting back in the car. It was difficult to tell, but it looked like that white thing wasn't in his back pocket anymore.

He left something in my office.

And I'm pretty sure Jackson knows what it was and where to find it.

"Fuck."

Nazmi popped his head in. "Pide is ready. You finished with that?"

"Can I get a copy of this?"

"Get a thumb drive, and it's yours." He handed me a small pizza box. "Lunch crowd is coming, so I've got to get back to it. If you're finished?"

"I'm finished. Thanks."

The bell tinkled as I left, the door swinging shut behind me. I looked up at the camera again. I flipped the top of the box open and grabbed a piece of lunch as I walked along the sidewalk, looking at the cameras either directly in front of the doors of the neighbouring businesses or in the window looking out. Orwell would be delighted.

I popped into the shop next to Nazmi's. A

sewing and craft shop. I stuffed a piece of pide in my mouth and regretted not getting a drink to wash it down. I stood in front of the proprietor for what felt like twenty minutes as I tried to recover from a clump of jalapenos, tears streaming down my face.

The elderly woman patiently waited. "You okay, son? Can I get you a tissue?"

I nodded and grabbed a fistful of them to staunch the flow of tears and nasal leakage.

"Nazmi really piles the peppers on, doesn't he? What can I do for you?"

A squashed the tissues into a sodden ball, looked behind her counter for a trash bin and tossed them. "I had an unwelcome visitor the other night, and I was wondering if I could look at your security video." I pointed to the camera in the front window. "Maybe it picked something up that can help me in my investigation."

"I'd love to help you, Mac, but that thing hasn't worked for years."

I pointed again. "But the, ah, the red light is on."

She winked. "Don't tell anybody, okay? My grandson hooked the LED up to the power supply.

Cost me less than a buck in parts and a grandkid's labour. Fixing the system would put me back hundreds, maybe thousands. Sorry, I can't help."

"I don't imagine you saw anyone heading into my place the night before last?"

She was shaking her head before I was finished talking. "Sorry, Mac. Don't remember anything."

I nodded thanks and left, stuffing another piece of pide in my mouth. Nazmi was an artist. It was excellent. Maybe a little bit too heavy in the jalapeno department, but I asked for it.

I walked a little slower up the stairs to my office. Eating and walking challenged my coordination. I got to the top of the stairs and stopped. The door was partially open. Again.

Chapter Twelve

I closed the lid on the box, now only half full, and slowly pushed the door open. My weapon was in the gun safe. By rights, I should have backed off and called the police but fuck them. As the door swung through its arc, the wave of cheap cologne assaulted my nose.

"Alfie? What the fuck. Doesn't anyone respect privacy anymore?" He was sitting in my chair, feet on my desk. "Just make yourself at home, why don't you?"

He smiled at me and moved around the desk to my guest chair. "You'd think someone who spent almost twenty-five years in the police force and then chose a career as a private investigator would put better security in their office."

"So I've heard. What are you doing here so fast? You learn something?"

Alfie placed his briefcase on the desk. It looked like something my father used in 1976. Boxy, hard-sided piece of plastic. He flipped the two catches and opened the case. He pulled out two files and dropped them on my desk. He flipped one of them open and pushed it toward me.

I pushed it back. "Summarise."

"The bank has video."

"I already told you that. Exculpatory."

Alf grimaced and shook his head. "Not so much. The report says a security video from inside the bank shows you alone with the money. I haven't received a copy yet, but I've requested it."

"The only time I was alone in that room, the doors were locked from the outside. What's Jackson think, that I shoved nine money bags up my ass?"

"They only need to convince twelve easily manipulated citizens."

I exhaled. "Fine. What's the other file?"

"Just a status update on discovery. I still haven't determined what evidence they've gleaned from here."

"There will be a sheet of paper, maybe two, implicating me." I rubbed an eye with my thumb. "Fuck."

"How do you know?"

I told him about the video of the guy heading up to my apartment with a folded sheet of paper in his back pocket and the empty pocket when he came back down.

"Where'd you see this video?"

"Habib's place."

"Who?"

"Nazmi. Tabeesh. Great food. Tried it?"

"Is it halal?"

"What fucking difference does that make to you?"

"Just saying. How do you want me to work your defence?"

I waved him off. "Hang on a sec. We need a bit more info. Get the video. Find out what was planted by Jackson's tools, and then we'll start talking about defence.

"I'll keep working on that. But it's not like we've got a lot of time."

I rested my forehead on my desk. Suddenly enormously tired. "Take a step backward. I need to find out who is framing me and why. Figure that out, and I can figure out how to undo it."

"I thought you were pegging Jackson as the go-to guy for this."

I waved away that suggestion. "I don't like the guy. That's not enough reason to hate him that much."

Alf slid both files back into his briefcase. "What did he ever do to you?"

"Oh, no. It was something I did to him. I banged his wife. He caught me. Us. In their hot tub. Not a pretty scene."

"Recently?"

"Hell no. Seven or eight years ago. That's why I keep giving him a hard time about Davey's parentage. It could have conceivably been me. See what I did there? Conceivably."

"So that's why you and Jane split?"

I waggled my hand. "Not so much. She found out after we separated. Pretty sure Jackson gave me up. He's never forgiven me." I smiled. "But it was worth it. That woman could suck the red off an apple."

"On that note, I'm gone. I'll keep at it. You stay out of trouble."

My ass. "Sure thing."

I waited until he left and took my windfall cheque to the bank. I slipped past Sophie and sat in the chair across from the junior loan manager, the one I had interrupted during a stressful telephone conversation.

I fumbled the cheque from my wallet and slid it across to him with my ATM card. "Deposit this in savings, please. Double-check that it isn't rubber first."

The kid looked at the issuer—the very bank we were sitting in—and grinned.

"I'm serious, kid. Make sure the bank is good for it. I understand a large sum of money is missing."

He stammered for a second, then slid the cheque

back to me. "You can take this to a teller, and they will handle it for you."

I slid it back to him. "I know you can do this. I know you can. By the way, well done on not getting your legs broken by your bookie."

His hand stopped an inch above the cheque. "How in the hell would you know anything about that?"

"I'm a detective. It's my job to know more than you. Deposit the cheque."

He scowled and filled in the deposit slip, banked the cheque and gave me a receipt with my card. I stored the deposit slip and my ATM card and handed him one of my business cards.

He looked at it closely, flipping it over a couple of times to see if there was anything on the back. Maybe he thought, after the first time, a rapid flip would catch something or someone out. There was nothing on the back. I'm cheap.

"What's this for?"

"I thought for a second you might have been involved with the robbery. You're clearly not, but if you need help with your bookie, call me. I probably know him."

He fished his wallet out of the inside pocket of his jacket and stowed the business card. "Thanks. I think."

"Is Harris free? I've got to talk to him for a second, if that's okay."

He opened his mouth to answer when Sophie glided in to take me by the elbow. "He's on a phone call right now, Mac. Come with me and sit at my desk. I'll fit you in when he's finished."

I sat on the corner of her desk and basked in her beauty for a second. "So, who do you think did it? I'm assuming you're one of the ones who think I'm innocent of all charges?"

She looked up at me, a squint on her face, which didn't detract from her looks at all. "He's available. Follow me."

She led me into the office, then left and closed the door behind her. I collapsed onto the hyper-comfortable sofa.

He studied me from his desk. "Surprised to see you here, all things considered."

I swung my feet onto the sofa and laid back, my

head on the armrest. "Surprised to see you still employed, all things considered."

He grunted and opened a side drawer on his desk, and retrieved two glasses. He poured a healthy serving of scotch in each, got up from his desk and walked around to me. He handed one to me, and I rotated to the sitting position. He sat across from me and took a large mouthful of the drink. I looked at mine and put it on the table between us leaving a ring on the glass tabletop.

Harris put his glass down on a coaster. "Stinks you had to spend time in jail, but you're out now. And we're clear. I vouched for you. You vouch for me."

I slid my drink a little further away from me. "You? What about Terry? Don't I vouch for him, too?"

"Him too, of course."

"Where is he?"

"I gave him the day off. Corporate has been chewing me a new asshole. I know Terry wants my job, and it seemed prudent to keep him away from the bloodbath."

I leaned back on the sofa and smiled. "You're freaking out, aren't you?"

"Who wouldn't? Why aren't you? You spent the night locked up. What do they have on you?"

I pushed myself up. "For that, I need to talk to Jackson."

Harris walked back to his desk chair. "Good luck with that. He absolutely hates you. Venomous."

I closed his office door as I left and tapped on Sophie's desk. "You see Terry today?"

"Harris told me he gave him the day off."

"Right. You keep your gorgeous eyes peeled for me, okay? The last guy in the bank who took a day off ended up getting beat to death."

Chapter Thirteen

The police station barely rated as one. It was small, a satellite office with the Lake Macquarie Local Area Command pulling the strings. I used to work out of the LM LAC, and my interactions with this group were always interesting, especially when Jackson was involved.

I pushed the front door open and stood at the counter—something like the counter you see when you go into a medical centre. It was almost chest-high and overlooked a few desks. It had the feel of an old Roads and Maritime office, and if not for the guns on the belts, it could be easily confused for such.

The faces at the desks continued working as if I wasn't there. I rapped on the countertop. "Where's Jackson?"

Nothing.

I rapped again, a little bit harder. "Anybody? Looking for that fat fuck Jackson."

A somewhat familiar face looked up from her desk, looked at me, and then at the door to one of the interview rooms. "I think he's busy."

"I'll wait."

The interview must have been over because the door opened, and Jackson, in all his sweaty glory, waddled out. He had the same polyester suit that he always seemed to be in, stressed at the seams and shiny in places it shouldn't be. His collar was frayed to the point any normal human being would have thrown the shirt in the bin, or used it to wash their truck. But he never washed his truck, so that's not something he would ever consider.

He had a smug-looking smile on his face. "Are you here to turn yourself in?" His body odour preceded him as he opened the gate at the counter and came out to the waiting area.

I took a half step back. "You know I didn't do it. Why are you setting me up? What's in it for you?"

He stood in front of me in a parody of every cop in every cop show you've ever seen. Feet shoulder-width apart, thumbs hooked in his belt on either side of the buckle. "You've got a history of light fingers, pal. Five years ago—"

"Nah, get fucked. You set me up for that evidence room thing. Put stuff in my apartment. And I was cleared."

"And left the force. Sure sign of guilt."

"No way I was willing to work on a force that stooped low enough to employ you."

He took a step forward and leaned in. "Get the fuck out of here before I pound you into a greasy spot on the floor."

I fought the gag reflex and moved closer to him. Nose to nose, stomach to stomach. "You've got a history of police brutality, Jackson. Nobody in here would be surprised." I took an unhealthy amount of pleasure in the shades of red that passed over his face.

I took a couple of steps back. "I'll see myself out. Nothing useful is happening here."

I unlocked the door to my office and flicked on the lights. It stayed light a little bit later, but by seven, it was well and truly dark. I dropped the keys and my phone on my desk and plugged in the kettle. I had dropped into my desk chair, stretching out my legs, when the power went out, stopping the kettle and plunging my place into darkness.

"Shit." I did a quick mental inventory—electricity bill paid, rent paid—this wasn't expected. I unlocked my phone and was scrolling for the power company's after-hours number when the door smashed open. The street lights provided enough illumination to see two men in balaclavas power in.

I got in front of one of them, and he connected with a haymaker. The tip of my chin. I didn't pull my head back fast enough. I spun onto the floor and rolled to my hands and knees. "Jesus. Was it something I said?"

I pushed myself to my feet. "What the fuck? Take whatever you want and get the hell out of here."

The haymaker guy got me with a couple of body blows and backed me into a corner. I kept my fists up by my head, elbows tucked tight to my body, doing a damned good job imitating Ali's "rope a dope" strategy. It worked better for him. The guy was getting most of his shots through. Thank God the second guy was busy trashing my computer, or I would have been in real trouble.

I swung a wild kick at the guy in front of me, catching him under the knee. He swore, took a step back, and then advanced. And his buddy came with him. Both of them were taking me apart. I slid to the floor in the foetal position, trying to cover up all the important bits as they laid a couple of kicks into me.

They stopped long enough for my new friend to spray "Back the fuck off" through the little hole in his balaclava, then added a couple more kicks for good measure before they ran out of the room and down the stairs.

I stayed on the floor for a few minutes, trying to catch my breath through the sharp pain of probably broken ribs. I heard a vehicle start, a throaty muffler and a screaming engine as it left. It sounded a lot like what the truck on Nazmi's security video would sound like.

I sniffed. A lingering smell I couldn't quite put my finger on. I rolled to my hands and knees and winced as I stood. They'd left my phone alone, so I turned on the built-in light and headed down the stairs and around to the back of the building. My car was still there, and there were fresh rubber trails from the arseholes peeling out. Fucking hoons.

I lifted the lid to the breaker box and flipped the switch back on for my apartment. It hurt to lift my arm. Never was much of a fighter. You didn't have to be when you had a shoulder holster and a badge. I'm getting too fat for this shit.

I limped back up the stairs, truly regretting the lack of a lift. A ground-floor office was in the cards.

The kettle was starting to boil, unaware that it had been interrupted. My old desktop computer, though, was smashed. Pulverised. The guy must have put his heel to any piece larger than a coffee cup. I spotted the hard drive among the rubble and bent down, gasping with the pain, and pulled it out of the mess. Maybe I'd find somebody who could retrieve the important bits.

It took a bit of cleaning and a dollop of scotch in

my coffee to ward off the pain enough to get the place back to a half-decent state. Sometime after eight, there was a light rap on the door, and Alfie poked his head in.

"Can I come in?"

"Sure. Why not?" I sat behind my desk and took a pad of paper and a pen from the centre drawer.

Alf sat across from me, his eyes flitting around the room. Then he stared at my face for a minute. "You get burgled?"

"How can you tell?"

"Pieces of computer under your desk. No computer *on* your desk. The bruise on your chin. The general state of mess this place is in." He held up his hands. "Although that last bit may just be normal you." He looked at my chin again. "You got jumped. In here."

"They hit like soccer players." I gently touched the bruise on my chin. "Get a copy of the video on Nazmi's security system. I'd give you good odds it was them. About the same size, and their vehicle sounded like what that truck should sound like."

"You get a look at them?"

"Balaclavas. Get videos from shops on either side of Nazmi's, too. If they've got it."

Alf wrote a note on his phone. "Think that'll help?"

"The two were talking to someone off-camera. Maybe we can see who it was." I looked at the empty spot on my desk. I hated that computer, but now I missed it. "I need a machine."

"I've got an old iMac I can lend you. Anything else?"

I ran my fingers through my hair and winced. I lifted my shirt and looked at the bruises along my ribs.

"Jesus, Mac."

I nodded. "Yeah. I better get these checked out." I lowered my shirt. "And no, I have no idea what the fuck they wanted."

"Let the cops know."

"I was just there. Came home to this. I'll give them a pass if that's okay with you."

Chapter Fourteen

Driving with cracked ribs is not as easy as you might imagine. I'm assuming they're cracked. Whenever I turned the steering wheel or shifted gears, it felt like something was grinding, particularly on the right side, up by my armpit. The guy had a hell of a left jab on him.

And if driving was difficult, getting out of the car once I got to the regional hospital was fucking near impossible. I swung my feet out first, placing them flat on the ground and slowly pushed myself forward until just the edge of my ass was on the seat. I slowly stood, taking shallow breaths, and a very long time.

Walking in was a piece of cake after that.

The triage nurse took my details and offered me a seat with the dozen other visitors. I didn't pay much attention to them. My focus was directed completely at the closest seat, which I collapsed into as soon as I reached it.

I tipped my head back and closed my eyes. Slow breaths in through the nose and out the mouth seemed to moderate the pain. Any position I placed my right arm in was bad, but some were worse than others. I finally adjusted it so the stress on my ribs was minimised, and the triage nurse appeared in front of me with a small paper cup full of pills and a plastic glass of water.

I took them, dropped them down my throat and handed the cups back to the nurse. "What were they?"

"Pain killers. It should help a bit. You're favouring—"

"—my entire right side. Yeah. Any idea how long I'll be? I'm pretty sure there's a couple of broken ribs."

"There are still a couple in front of you." She did

a quick visual survey of the crowd in the waiting room. "Why don't I send you to X-Ray now? Save a little bit of time." She stepped away for a second, then returned with a clipboard full of forms. She spoke while she filled it in. "Have you seen Jane yet?"

I shook my head. "Didn't know she was working tonight. Would have gone to Gosford if I knew she was here."

She tucked the clipboard under her arm. "I think you two should work it out. I always thought you guys made a great couple."

I raised my eyebrows. "You've actually met her, right?"

She scribbled something on the bottom of the form and handed it to me. "Take this to X-Ray. Follow the blue line on the floor, and you can't miss it." She winked. "Maybe if you're lucky, you'll bump into her."

I don't know if you'd call it lucky. I think she was lying in wait. I turned the corner to the small waiting area by radiology and, at first, registered just a single person ahead of me. Then I registered *who* it was. "Ah, Christ. What the hell is this?"

Jane looked up from the three-year-old magazine she was reading. She had a huge smile on her face. "I hear you've been pummelled. Serious, I hope?"

"Don't worry. I'm not going anywhere. You'll still get your monthly cheque." I would have willingly delivered it in bags of five-cent coins.

She looked shocked. "Mac. Really, now. I'm concerned for your health. You're getting too old to put the dukes up. Weren't you the one preaching to me to never fight back in a mugging? Just give them what they want, you said."

"It would appear that what they wanted was to beat the shit out of me. Are you going to stay here and hassle me all night? I thought you had actual medical-type work to do."

She stood and patted me on the stomach. I reflexively pulled it in and winced as the stress was transferred to my ribs. "Shit."

"Oh, wow, Mac. So sorry."

"Bullshit, I think."

A radiology tech exited a lead-lined room. "Malcolm Durridge?"

I raised my left hand a couple of inches.

"This way, sir." He nodded at Jane. "Doctor."

"Take care of yourself, Mac. You're not getting any younger."

"Neither are you," I yelled, but the door was closed by then, so I doubt she heard me.

I walked out of the hospital almost three hours later, pushing midnight. I was a little more upright and in a little less pain. My torso was strapped like I was heading to a fancy dress ball as King Tut. In my shirt pocket was a packet of pain pills. Enough to last me until I get to the chemist.

I had parked in a two-hour zone. Three hours ago. I pulled the parking ticket off my window, swore another curse at the local constabulary and eased myself into the car. I fished the packet of pills out of my shirt pocket, broke the seal on two of them and dry swallowed. They couldn't kick in fast enough.

The drive home was uneventful, but only because there were no other cars on the road. I crossed the centre line half a dozen times and bounced off the centre circle of two different roundabouts. Definitely not in top form.

I stood at the bottom of the thirty-seven stairs and contemplated sleeping in my car for the night. Common sense prevailed, though. It might be a long climb up, but the reward of a comfy bed would more than pay for it. Sleeping in my Corolla would probably be the worst thing I could do with my ribs.

I had some momentum going when I got to the top and hit the doorknob without breaking stride. Which would have been fine if the door hadn't been locked. My face hit the door first, protecting my ribs.

"Shit. Fuck. Ouch." I unlocked and eased myself in and flicked on the light.

An older vintage iMac sat on my desk, screen black. I walked to my side of the desk and read the note taped to the screen: *I locked the door for you. You probably already figured that out. Use this computer until you sort something else out. The videos from the shops have already been loaded on it. I'll call you in the morning. Alf.*

What a guy.

I pulled the note off the screen and looked for the rest of the computer and the power button. There was a monitor, a keyboard, and a mouse plugged into the back of the monitor. It took me a few minutes, but I finally found the power button on the bottom back of the monitor and flashed the computer up.

While it cycled through whatever it had to cycle through, I poured myself a neat double scotch. I dropped it down my throat and poured another.

I sat in front of the computer, looking at the unfamiliar interface. The mouse moved the cursor so that, at least, was the same. The screen looked a bit wobbly, though, and now there were two cursors. I blinked a couple of times and squinted at the monitor. The whole image was out of focus.

I blinked again, then had a thought. I pulled the packet of pills out of my pocket. A label across the back of the box, in large red letters, read: *Warning. May cause drowsiness. Do not consume with alcohol.*

"Fuck."

My last memory of that night was of the keyboard rapidly advancing to my face.

Chapter Fifteen

Returning to consciousness was a slow and painful process. I sat slumped over in my chair, face on my keyboard and a line of spittle from the corner of my mouth to the desk. The dull ache that throbbed in my head was immediately put into perspective when I tried to sit upright. Red-hot daggers pierced my ribs, and I almost returned to unconsciousness. I would have welcomed it.

I pushed myself away from my desk and gritted my teeth. I wiped my mouth with my sleeve and looked for the packet of pain pills. On the floor. Shit.

I scrambled around for a few minutes before

finally getting my hands on them and downing two.

I eased off my shirt and looked at the strapping. The doc didn't mention anything about it being waterproof, but I needed a shower. Really needed a shower. I guess a field test was in order.

It wasn't, really. Water-proof, that is. Some of it loosened around the edges, but it still supported the damage. It didn't dry, though, so I had a band of wet on my shirt when I left for The Pelican. I needed coffee. I don't think I could handle food.

I think I walked like an old man with a load of shit in his pants. It felt like I did. I eased into a booth near the window, and Jessie dropped a menu on my table.

"Coffee?" she asked.

"Does the pope shit in the woods?"

"So that would be no?"

"That would be yes. This particular pope shits in the woods." I took a shallow breath. "Your largest, strongest cup of coffee, please." I handed the menu back to her. "No food today. Stomach's a bit off."

She tucked the menu under her arm. "You find the asshole who killed Jimmy yet?"

I looked up at her. "You going to bring me my coffee?"

"Asshole."

"Look, Jess, I'm not a cop anymore. That's a police matter. Hassle them."

"You'd think you'd be looking."

I shook my head. "You would, would you? You'd be wrong."

"Some fucking detective you are."

"I heartily agree. Please bring my coffee."

I rested my elbows on the table and pushed the heels of my hands into my eyes. I was so tired. At least the pain pills were working. Something had to. I took a slightly deeper breath, testing the limits of pain in my chest. And then a deeper one still. All good until the narcotics wear off.

My reverie was disturbed by someone sliding into the booth across from me. I removed my hands from my eyes, blinked away the spots and focussed on Jackson. Oh, well. A shitty day just got worse.

"Hear you got the shit kicked out of you."

"Get fucked, Jackson. I'm trying to enjoy a peaceful breakfast."

He grabbed a couple of tubes of sugar, ripped the ends off and poured them down his throat. He swallowed and smiled. "Really sorry."

"Really?"

"Yeah. Really sorry it wasn't me pounding on you." He chuckled. The guy had an IQ just north of a brick.

"You're lucky it wasn't. You, I can take."

He jerked forward and slapped both palms on the table, making a noise loud enough to wake a drunk. I'm sure Barry didn't appreciate it. "Maybe next time, it *will* be me."

I took a deep breath. At least as deep as I could make it. "Listen, mate, it was over seven years ago. Let it go. I have. Why can't you? Sure, I fucked your wife, but believe me, I wasn't the only one."

His eyes narrowed. I couldn't take him today. Not with these ribs.

"Just relax, okay? Water under the bridge. I've forgiven you."

"What, the evidence room thing? That was just going to be a prank until I found out you were banging my wife. In my hot tub. Gave it a little extra juice after that."

"And I ended up under investigation for a shit load of stuff missing. Cleared, mind you. You're not that clever." I cocked my head at him. "Forced me to resign, and now I'm the happiest I've ever been. The best thing that ever happened to me."

Jackson leaned forward. "Doubt that."

"Why are you here?"

He took another sugar tube from the bowl on the table and tipped it down his throat. "I heard about your incident yesterday."

"I'm touched."

He nodded at my right side. "They did all that damage in less than a minute? You're not the Mac I knew."

"You're still the Jerk-Off Jackson I always knew." Jesus, I've got to stop antagonising the cops. But I can't help it with this guy.

He ignored me. "Was it just the one? Or was there a gang of them?"

I pushed the bowl of sugar packets closer to him. "Have another. Diabetes looks good on you." I watched him for a second. "Hey, do you know anyone who owns a black ute? Noisy exhaust?"

He crumpled another packet and dropped it on the table. "Lotsa trucks like that around here."

"They smelled like friends of yours."

Jackson farted, smiled and stood. "Like that?" He grabbed a couple more packets of sugar and walked out.

Jessie picked that time to come by with my coffee. She wrinkled her nose as she entered Jackson's emission. "Jesus, Mac. What the hell?"

I pointed at the closing door. "That wasn't me. That belongs to..." I shook my head. "Never mind. Look, about Jimmy. I'm really sorry what happened. The cops are looking at it, I'm sure, but I'll keep my eyes open, okay?"

Her eyes glistened. "Thanks."

"So, what have you heard?"

"Probably the same as you."

"Except he was talking to you Monday morning. Was he sick then?"

She frowned at me like I was a moron. "No. Why would he be sick?"

"Harris said he called in sick. Headed to the

beach, I guess, where he was beat on." I shrugged. "It was a beautiful day. He didn't mention anything to you about pulling a sickie?"

She shook her head. "He was hitting on me like usual. The poor guy."

I chewed the inside of my cheek. A difficult subject to broach, and I didn't want waterworks. I sighed. It had to be asked. "I thought you didn't like him, what with you giving him the bum's rush all the time. You never did go out with him, did you?"

Her chin started that 'I'm going to cry now' quiver. Damn. She sniffed and managed to keep the tears at bay. "I liked fucking with his head. If I'd known that—" and that's all she wrote. The tears started flowing, and she ran back to the kitchen in full sob. Double-damn.

I sipped my coffee, waiting patiently for the caffeine kick I so desperately needed. It felt like it was going to be a shitty day, and the third in a row. Fuck.

Then the bell tinkled above the door, and Alf walked in, a sour look on his face. Guaranteed the third shit day in a row, I guess.

Chapter Sixteen

"You look like a bucket of old shit."

"Awesome. And thanks. What the fuck are you doing here?"

He waved in the general direction of the register for a menu and slid across from me. "Breakfast. Seeing you here saves me a trip after."

Jessie dropped a menu in front of him, scowled at me and headed back to the kitchen. I had a feeling service would be poor today.

"And you wanted to see me, why?"

"How's the ribs?"

I reflexively touched my right side and coughed,

wincing and gritting my teeth at the same time. "Lovely. Yours?"

"I'm the picture of health. Broken, cracked or bruised?"

"One straight up broken and two cracked." I took a breath and eased it out. "And all bruised. I miss the good old days when I could count on my friends in blue to roust these fuckers and lay a bit of a beating on them before they brought them in."

"I didn't hear that, Mac."

Jessie came back to the table, a little more presentable but still favouring me with a stink-eye. She stood there with an order pad, pen poised above it, saying nothing.

Alf looked up at her. "Oh, yeah. Skim latte and an omelette. Ham, tomato and cheese. Sourdough toast, too, if you've got it."

My stomach rumbled. Maybe food wouldn't be a bad idea. "Same for me. Except for the coffee. I've got my coffee."

She spun on her heel and strode back to the kitchen. I don't know if she wrote down my order or if I'd even get anything. If she showed up with Alf's food only, I would steal his toast.

"She seems pissed."

"Not happy that I'm not looking into Jimmy. I told her I wasn't a cop anymore."

"Not good enough, mate."

I arched my back a little to pull the ribs apart. A little. Breathing was a bit easier, but it would be a long haul. "So you just wanted to see me to see how the ribs were? Very kind of you."

Jessie put his coffee in front of him, and he nodded thanks. "Not just that, my friend. How's my computer working?"

"No idea. I passed out in front of it last night, just after I figured out how to turn it on. I'll get back to it later." I sipped coffee. "Thanks, though. Never used one of them before. It might take a little while to figure it out."

"Nah, piece of piss. Give it a try, and if you've got any problems, give me a call. I can walk you through it."

Jess slid a plate in front of Alf, then an identical one in front of me. I took a sniff, and my stomach grumbled again. "Thanks, Jessie. Smells great."

"I'll let mom know."

I took a bit of toast and a mouthful of omelette and tried talking to Alf at the same time. "You see anything on the videos?"

Alf laughed and swallowed. "What the fuck was that, man?"

I guess it came out like 'Yuff see abiding onnabideo?'.

I swallowed and sipped coffee. "I said, did you see anything on the videos?"

He shrugged. "I don't think so. I watched them, but other than the front end of that ute, nothing much."

"So enlighten me. You're billing me at some ungodly amount per hour to check on my ribs and tell me the evidence you grabbed for me was useless?"

"Pretty much." He smiled as he sipped his coffee. "Well, maybe one more thing."

I looked at him, waiting.

"You want me to tell you?"

"No, I want to read your fucking mind. Yes. Tell me."

"The two guards who moved your cash are

working again this morning. Different banks, different places, but if I were you, I'd be watching their activity. If it wasn't Harris, Terry or you, it would have to be them."

I pushed my plate back. "Right. Where are they?"

"Right now? Not sure. But they'll be doing a pickup at a different branch, same bank, in about an hour."

I patted my pockets until I found my notepad and pen. I slid them across the table at him, a little forcefully, I think. "Address."

"Jesus. Relax, man." He wrote in the small notebook and pushed it and the pen back to me. "By all means, go check them out, but don't get into a fight with them. It won't help, and it'll look bad for you when you get to court."

I grabbed the paper and made for the door. "Pay for my breakfast, will you Alf? I'll pay you back someday."

Jessie's athletic skills were on full display. She made it from behind the till on the other side of the cafe to between me and the door in the space of time it took me to hobble a couple of steps from the booth.

She put her hand on my chest, and damn, but it hurt. Almost brought to my knees by an almost waif teen. She pulled her hand back and mirrored my wince. "Oh, jeez. Sorry, Mac. I didn't think."

I put on that brave male face that refuses to sob in pain in front of a beautiful female. "Nothing. It's nothing." I think that's what I said. My teeth were clenched pretty hard. I wiggled my jaw loose. "Why did you stop me? I've got an appointment I really need to get to." I made like I was going to push past her, and she put her hand up near my chest. That's all it took. The proximity of the hand to the bruises was enough to stop me. "What, Jessie, is that important?"

"I'm really sorry for getting all bitchy and stuff, and I really want to know if you can investigate who killed Jimmy because even though I gave him a really hard time, I really, really liked him."

Really. Those words poured out of her mouth like rain down a spout. Her chin quivered, and water was pooling in her eyes. Shit. "I'll do what I can, Jess. No promises, okay? If I get in the cops' way, they'll pull me up. For something. I'm not on the best terms with them."

She went to tap me on the chest again, and I caught her by the wrist. "Yeah, don't do that. I hurt. And you're welcome, okay?" She nodded, a small smile cracking her face, and walked back to the till.

Chapter Seventeen

It took me a little while to find them. It's not like a big grey truck and two armed guards could hide, at least not easily, but Alf gave me the wrong address. I expected better from a solicitor. I think everyone does.

But I found them. Right in front of my face, eventually. A good six blocks from where they were supposed to be, on the main drag out in front of the bank.

Too much walking.

Sweat layered my face and the large part of my skull that was balding. A little endorphin action kept the pain down, but it was illusory. I'd be hurting later.

Guard number one—the one who stood by the truck like a drugstore Indian when they were behind the bank—was unlocking the back of the truck when I approached. I guess they switched off on the duties, which made good sense.

I got within a metre of him before he noticed me. I could have pulled his weapon from its holster, and there's nothing he could have done about it.

I didn't. I'm a nice guy, deep down. "Hey, boys."

The guy at the truck slapped his hand on his sidearm and spun, his other hand outstretched toward me. I took a quick step back and put my hands up in surrender. "Whoa, boss. Take it easy."

His narrowed eyes were, I suppose, meant to convey some kind of menace. He looked like a pig in the sun. "Ya shouldn't be that close, mate."

I shrugged, instantly regretting it. "Yeah." I eased out a breath. "You should maybe pay more attention."

The other guard came to life. He moved away from his designated 'cover' position and closer to us. "Hey."

"Hey, right back at ya."

"You're the guy what robbed that other bank."

"Use 'allegedly', or I'll sue for libel. Or slander. Whichever fits."

"You looking to fatten your bank balance even more?"

I wagged a finger at him. "Careful, buddy." Both of them were within spitting distance. "Strikes me that the people with the best opportunity to skim that cash are standing right in front of me."

There's a disadvantage to standing that close. The first guy gave me a shove in the chest. The endorphins weren't up to the task. I staggered a step back, holding up my hand. "Come on, guys. I'm injured. And old. Take it easy on me. I'm just taking the piss, okay?" I took a deep breath. "But it's a reasonable assumption, though, right?"

"We found out about the pickup the morning of. You think we're smart enough to plan something like this on that short notice?"

I love being fed a good straight line. I nodded. "You're absolutely right. No way you two are smart enough to pull this off. Not even remotely possible."

The first guy started coming for me and the 'cover' guy put out an arm and stopped him. Thank God.

"Enough of this. We've got this job to do. You've got the fucking back open, and we're distracted. They talked about this in the morning meeting, right?" He slapped his companion on the back. "Pull your head in." He slid back to the cover spot and kept an eye on the surroundings.

"Guys, I'm just trying to figure out what happened."

"What happened is that you robbed a place. *Now*, you're trying to figure out how to blame someone else. Specifically me." The guard turned back to the truck. He lifted a trolley down and put a couple of cases on it. "Or us."

"I already crossed you two off the list. Intellectual shortcomings."

"Huh?"

"Exactly." I scratched at my jaw while he placed two more cases on the trolley. "Who arranged the pickup?"

"This one?" The guy locked the back of the truck

and pushed the trolley toward the front of the bank.

"No, you..." Best not to say what I was thinking. "The one on Monday where I was framed for the robbery."

"What about it? Hurry it up, mate. We're busy."

"Who arranged the pickup for Monday?"

"The bank did. The bank always does."

"Fucking obviously. Who at the bank arranged it?"

"How the hell would I know? We're horses cocks..."

"Yeah. Right. You go where you're shoved." I looked up at the front of the bank. "You always pick up at the back?"

"Obviously not. We're delivering to the front right now."

Oh, my God, those guys were thick. "No, buddy. Do you always do your pick-ups for the bank on Monday at the back?"

He stopped pushing the trolley and expended some energy thinking. "No, actually, now that you mention it, that was out of the ordinary. Huh." He resumed pushing.

I let him go. Doubtful that I could get anything more than that out of him. "You've both been a great help. As you were."

I turned for the long walk back to my car and spotted Jackson leaning against his car. He slid his sunglasses down his nose and winked at me.

I flipped him the bird and turned away. Didn't need to go toe-to-toe with him right now. I *wanted* to, but it would have to wait.

I gave Alfie a call.

"Mac, where are you?"

"Just had a chat with the cabbage-head twins. All they're good for is pushing trolleys around."

"They the ones who beat on you?"

"No. The two thugs had a smell. Sunscreen, salt water and bad B.O. Probably surf a lot. The guards have too much ballast to be surfies." I checked over my shoulder. Jackson had gotten in his car. "Alf, buddy, I need that footage from the bank."

"I keep pressing, but they're dragging their heels on this for some reason."

"You keep trying the legit way, and I'm going to try an end-run. Get an external hard drive and meet me in an hour. The Pelican. You can buy me lunch."

"What's the hard drive for?"

"Get one, okay? I'm sure you'll bill me."

Chapter Eighteen

I needed new shoes. I was walking too much, and my feet were killing me. I popped into the bank. Time to end run Jackson. I stood in the lobby for a second, formulating a plan. Then, I decided to wing it because my plans rarely turned out how I wanted them to.

I slid into the chair across from Sophie's desk. "Got a minute?"

She paused typing something in a spreadsheet and looked up from the papers on her desk. "Not really." She sighed and smiled at the same time. "But I could use a break. What's up?"

I leaned forward and crossed my arms on her

desk. I winced at the stab of pain and closed my eyes for a second. I took a deep breath in through my nose—as deep as I could manage—and let it out slowly. "I need a hand." I checked for any eavesdroppers and then spoke quietly. "My lawyer and I are getting the run-around from the cops. Probably Jackson, specifically. I need a copy of the security system video from the backroom for all of Monday."

She was shaking her head before I even got to 'I need'. "There are policies, procedures and permissions, authorisations for—"

I put my hand on her arm and stopped her. "Do you believe I robbed this place?"

She looked at Harris' closed door, chewed at her lip for a second, then shook her head. "No. I don't think so."

"*Think?*"

"Okay, no. I do not believe you robbed the bank."

I patted her arm and nodded. "Okay. Good. We're getting somewhere. I'm a dead man here. Jackson and his friends are hell-bent on burying me."

"I know what you did to Jackson."

Shit. "Years ago, and the asshole deserved it."

She shrugged and looked at Harris's office door again. "Maybe. Look, I don't know what you want me to do. An IT guy needs a formal request in the form of a warrant to proceed. Then he makes a digital copy of the security video and delivers it by registered post to the police department. Your solicitor *has* to get a copy from the police." She picked at her thumbnail. "I really don't know how I could help you."

"The video system is on the premises, right?"

She pointed at a door beside the one I went through, and shouldn't have, on Monday. "In there with the local server and phone switch. What are you thinking about doing?"

I sat back and spread my hands on her desk, looking at my splayed fingers. "It's probably a really good idea if you don't know too much."

Sophie raised an eyebrow. "You want to defend yourself against the accusation of robbing the bank by breaking into the bank? You've got a soft spot on your head, Mac."

I reflexively scratched at the back of my head.

"No. I'm not an idiot. At least not that much of one. You're working here tonight?" I held up my hands to stop her from answering me. "No, let me rephrase that. *Can* you be here tonight after hours? Some extra work you need to get done?"

"I don't know, Mac."

"You won't be doing anything illegal. Strictly speaking."

She narrowed her eyes. "I'm going to regret this. Aren't I?"

"I promise you, no." I went to stand, then reached for my wallet, took out my bank card and slid it across her desk. "Can you check my balance? I want to see if that cheque your boss gave me has cleared."

She slid the card through a reader and handed it back. She pointed at a numeric keypad on her desk. "Your pin?"

I tapped it in and sat back. I pride myself on being an excellent reader of peoples' body language, and something was pinging. Sophie looked at me, at her monitor and back at me again. I didn't need to be an expert on facial tics to read her expression. Something was wrong. "What?"

She frowned. "Well, your balance sure is healthy."

"So it cleared, then?"

"I don't think Harris paid you this much. I *know* he didn't." She spun her monitor around so I could see it.

There were two accounts displayed on the screen. "No, you've made a mistake, Soph. I've only got one account attached to this card. Not two. And Jesus, I definitely don't have that kind of money." I counted zeros with my finger. "Two hundred and fifty thousand dollars?" I dropped back in my chair. "No way."

"Yeah. It's in your name, but I don't think it's yours. You've never worked hard enough to make that kind of cash."

I took out my phone and opened my banking app. Entered the pin code and looked at the results. The one account with barely over a thousand in it.

I thought for a few seconds. This wasn't good. This was the exact opposite of good. This was going to royally fuck me. "I can't see it." I held up my phone so she could see the screen. "That account might be in my name, but I don't appear to have access to it." I pulled at my lip and looked at her screen again. "But I could withdraw all of it and there's nothing you could do about it, right?"

"It's in your name, Mac. But it's not yours. Even you're not that much of an ass."

"Hey, I'm just trying to figure this out. Can you print out when the deposits were made? The money had to get in there somehow."

She pulled the monitor back and tapped a couple of keys and pulled a piece of paper off her printer. "Looks like they have all been in the past two or three weeks."

I took the page from her and scanned through the entries. "If I stole the money Monday, how did I deposit it three weeks ago?"

"I don't know. It doesn't make any sense. Just like it makes no sense that you have a second account," she tapped some more keys, "that was opened the day before the deposits started."

I looked at the dates and times of the deposits again. "This says I was in here almost every day, and sometimes twice a day, making deposits. I clearly wasn't. I need video from the back *and* the last couple of weeks from the lobby area." Sophie nodded, and I folded the paper and slid it into my back pocket as I stood. "Tonight, okay?"

She nodded this time. No hesitation. "Of course. Anything else I can do to help, just ask."

I kissed her on the cheek. "Very much appreciated. I've still got things to do. I'll catch you later."

The cheek kiss was a spontaneous thing, but I think she liked it.

Chapter Nineteen

I needed some help. Some below-the-radar, invisible help. And I knew just the guy. Too many things were happening, all of them connected in one way or another, and I couldn't track them all. I rubbed my ribs. They weren't hurting as much. Not as much as they did yesterday. They still felt like I'd been at the bottom of a collapsed scrum. The last time I got in a fight I was fourteen. And I got my ass handed to me then, too.

You can't tell me that the two apes that jumped me aren't in some way related to all of this. Somebody sets me up for a bank robbery—a really strange bank robbery—and the regular security guy is killed. When I start sniffing into it just the tiniest amount, two thugs play drum line on my ribs. Yeah. Connected.

So I had to track them down at the same time I was kinda stealing video footage from the bank.

Barry was always free. And despite his personal situation, he's a pretty stand-up guy.

First, I needed a couple of things. A couple of blocks away, there was a chain electronics shop. I picked up a couple of pre-pay phones and paid for them with some of Ernie's cash—good old Ernie. I cracked open the packages and programmed the number of each phone into the others' contacts. Communications sorted.

Barry's currency of choice was food. Well, really, it was alcohol of any sort, but food was a close second. I ducked into the cafe and met Jess at the deli counter.

"You find out anything more about who killed Jimmy?"

"I need a BLT, Jess. On Turkish." She narrowed her eyes, and I could see her jaw muscles clenching. "I'm working on it, okay? Got a couple of good leads.

Hope to know more tomorrow."

"Sounds like a line to fob me off."

"Make me the sandwich, Jess. There's no fobbing going on. I'm actively working on it now. The sandwich will help."

"Yeah, right."

The only example in the English language of a double positive meaning a negative.

"Yeah. Right. And a couple of lattes. Double sugar in each."

She grumbled something and got to work. She prepared the lattes while the bread toasted. After ten minutes and a healthy tip that barely mollified her, I was leaving her shop with the electronics bag, a sandwich and a couple of take-away cups of coffee. Barry was where Barry always was. I sat down on the sidewalk beside him and handed him the bag of food and one of the coffees.

He opened the top of the bag and peered in. "What's this?"

"BLT, mate. How have you been?"

He looked at me, a little confused. "Weren't we just fishing, like not that long ago? I'm the same as I was then. Except a bit drier. You want something." He took the sandwich out and sniffed it. "A BLT? Little early for lunch."

"It's almost 5:00, buddy." His lack of time awareness was special. I wished, on many occasions, to be that oblivious about the time of day.

"I prefer these with a beer."

I fished the keys to my car out of my jacket pocket and handed them to him. "No beer today."

He took my keys and looked at them. "What's these for?"

"In a sec, Baz." I opened the bag from the electronics chain, took out the two pre-paid phones and handed him one.

He chuckled and placed it on the sidewalk between his feet. "Like I'm going to fucking use this." He took a sip of coffee. "Beer really would have been better." He tossed the keys back to me. "I don't have a driver's licence."

Stubborn old fuck. "Not a problem, Baz. What's the worst that could happen? You get picked up and spend a couple of weeks in the local lockup, warm and well-fed." I handed the keys back and closed his hand around them. "I really need your help."

He opened his hand and looked at the keys. "What's this about?"

"Jimmy was dumped at the beach, right? And the two fuckers who beat on me smelled like three-day-old sweat mixed with sea salt and weed. Surfers. I want you to head up to that beach, stash the car somewhere and keep an eye on the place. See if a couple of guys show in a black ute, one bald as a cue ball and the other stereotypically shaggy." I handed him the pre-paid phone. "And if they *do* show. Call me on this. The other number is already programmed in it. Real easy to use."

He grabbed it from me and scowled. "This is sounding more and more like work, Mac. I should be getting paid, right?"

"Haven't you heard? I robbed the bank. I've got millions stashed. Somewhere." I winked at him and pulled myself to my feet. "My car's behind my place. There should be enough petrol in it, but if there isn't," I pulled a fifty from Ernie's wad of cash, "this should do it."

The bill disappeared into one of his pockets fast

enough to impress Penn and/or Teller. He took a bite of the sandwich. "When you want me to do this?"

I looked at the time on my phone. "Any time after right now. The sooner, the better."

"It'll be dark. And cold."

"And it'll be dark and cold if you're here sitting on the sidewalk. Do me the favour, okay?"

He sipped at his coffee and smacked his lips. "Sure thing, Mac. As soon as I finish the BLT, I'm outta here."

"You're a champ, Baz. Now, if you'll excuse me, I've got to talk to a man about breaking into a bank."

Chapter Twenty

I left Baz to his BLT, which he seemed to be pornographically enjoying, and steered my way toward the pub. If I timed it right I'd get a beer in before Alf showed up. I can't remember the last time Alfie bought a round.

The pub was dark after the bright afternoon sun, and it took a minute for my eyes to adjust. It's one of those things that takes longer the older you get. I took a quick look around—no Alf. So I only needed to buy one. I grabbed a schooner of a low-carb variety. It's a waste of time, really, given the amount of junk food I eat, but we all lie to ourselves in different ways.

I think there is nothing much better than a cold beer on an early-season warm day. It's a commonplace joy during the heat of January, but a cold beer on the first warm day in August is something special.

I slid into a booth and took a fair draw on my drink. Alf slid into the bench seat across from me and dropped a package on the table. "Your hard drive. What's it for?"

I slid the sheet of paper Sophie had printed for me across the table. "What does this look like to you?"

He unfolded it and held at arm's length, squinting, then put on a pair of glasses. He skimmed over it quickly from top to bottom, then much slower, a frown creasing his forehead. "This is your account? Holy shit."

"That's what they say."

He looked at the bottom page, where the balance sat. "I'm not charging you enough." He looked over the top of his glasses at me. "Nowhere near enough."

I shook my head. "It's not mine, Alf. And that's the problem."

He ran his finger down the list of deposits. "Says here you've been depositing significant amounts of cash into that account over the past couple or three weeks."

I pointed at the package on the table. "And that's why I needed you to get the hard drive. It says they were counter deposits. In that branch. At first, I just needed a video from the back room on Monday, but I'm going to need the lobby footage for the past three weeks to prove I wasn't actually in there. I'm pretty sure evidence that shows I wasn't in the bank for any of these times should be enough proof of a frame job."

Alf stared at me for a few seconds, then shook his head. "Nope. Don't have a clue what you're talking about."

"You had any luck with Jackson getting the video?"

"No. You know that."

"Exactly. I've got a friend in the bank if you're up for a bit of felony-adjacent activity."

Alf sighed and dry scrubbed his face. "Fuck, mate. You shouldn't be telling me stuff like this."

"You're my lawyer. Who else can I tell? You going to help?" I nursed my beer. Wiped some of the condensation off and used the moisture trace rings on the table.

"The video is stored at the branch, I take it."

"At least a copy is. Like I said, I've got a friend who will help us get to it."

"That's going to implicate her, too. And none of it will be admissible."

I shrugged. It seemed like a stupid thing to say, but I wasn't going to tell my lawyer that. The video definitely wouldn't show me doing anything incriminating. I knew that for a fact. So, if it would clear me, there's no way it would incriminate me. "We just need to know what to ask for in discovery. And how did you know it was a 'her'?"

He smiled. "Good guess."

I pulled the hard drive out of its packaging. Alf bought me a 1 TB drive. It would hold months' worth of video—serious overkill. "You're going to charge me a lot for this, aren't you?"

He smiled and waved the sheet of paper at me. "You can afford it."

"Jesus."

He waved for a waiter and ordered a beer and a club sandwich. When the waiter left, he leaned forward with a smile. "You're paying, right?"

"When's the last time you bought me a beer, counsellor?"

"Trust me, Mac. Any time I buy anyone a beer, it ends up on their bill. Somewhere."

Alf's beer and sandwich arrived, and I tapped the rim of my glass for another. "Alf, my friend, we all know. Tell me, as a solicitor, have you ever experienced the kind of delays Jackson is pulling?"

He shook his head, then paused and thought for a minute. He took a sip of his beer and shook his head again. "No. This is abnormal. I have every right to go to the courts at the end of the week and compel him."

"Seem strange to you?"

Alf shook his head and then shrugged apologetically. "It's you. You boinked his wife. This is his opportunity to get you back."

I closed my eyes and leaned my head back. "He already got back to me. That's why I'm no longer a cop. Fucking asshole." I opened my eyes. "Not you."

"I know. Let's go get that video."

"I'm a bit of a technical idiot. You can do this?"

Alf dropped back the rest of his beer. "I can do it." He stood. "As long as we can get into the server room."

"I'm pretty positive we can. Just don't tell anyone."

"It won't be admissible."

"You said that already. Legal claptrap. I don't care if it's admissible. I need something to shove down Jackson's throat."

Chapter Twenty-One

The sun had slipped below the horizon, and the temperature had dropped by a hell of a lot more than I was comfortable with. I shoved my hands in my pockets and trotted across the street to the bank.

Alf was half a dozen steps behind me. "What's the rush, Mac?"

"You're kidding, right?" I stopped in front of the bank and knocked on the glass door, but not hard. Sophie's ears still worked just fine.

Alf caught up and tucked in beside me. "We're standing in front of the bank at night, acting kinda suspicious. You got this?"

I saw Sophie come out of a back room. "Yeah, I got this."

She punched a code into the alarm panel by the door, unlocked it at its base and opened it for us. "Quickly."

I ducked in, Alf on my heels. Sophie poked her head out, looked up and down the sidewalk, closed the door, locked it and reset the alarm. Six easy-to-remember digits.

She ushered us out of the lobby and into Harris' office.

"What are we doing in here?" I looked for his pen. It wasn't on his desk. Maybe next time.

Sophie looked out of the office toward the front of the bank. "Don't want anybody seeing you in here, Mac. Why are you here, Alf?"

Shit. I should have told her he was coming along. "I'm not a technical giant, Soph. Alf has the abilities, I have the need, and you have the," I hesitated. "No. Let's not involve you any more than is necessary. Just show us where the server is and go back to whatever you used as an excuse to stay late."

She kept her head out the door, watching street

traffic in front of the bank. "It's kinda late now, Mac. I'm in it up to my ears. Do what you need to do and get out of here as fast as you can."

She left the door and walked behind Harris' desk, pulling a pass card from the centre drawer. She poked her head out the door, looked over her shoulder and motioned for us to follow. She entered a "Staff Only" door secured by a card reader. Sophie swiped Harris' card, and the red light on the reader turned green. She smiled and pushed open the door, and we slipped into a room not much larger than a closet.

I looked at her with a little more respect. "You've just done Harris in, haven't you? If anything shit comes from this."

She waggled the card and smiled. "I was never here."

I smiled back and shook my head, then looked around the room. There were three computers in a rack—servers, if you asked the IT guys—all powered from a UPS and with no monitors or keyboards. Separate from that was a desktop computer plugged in to the wall with a very old monitor and a keyboard that was probably manufactured in the late 90s.

Sophie grabbed a stapler off the desk and propped the door open a crack. "It gets warm in here with the door closed."

Alf was already sitting at the small desk and had the external drive plugged into a USB port on the desktop. He tapped the spacebar on the keyboard, and the screen came to life. "No password? Not very secure."

"The security is the door, Alf," said Sophie. "It's secure enough."

"We're here, so not that secure," I said. "Alf, what do you have?"

He finger-pecked the keyboard with a speed I've rarely seen from Alfie. "I'm copying all the videos from the past month. We can filter later. It'll take a few minutes to get it all, but that's a lot faster than trying to find specific time ranges." He pecked a couple more keys. He was reaching for the cable to unplug the hard drive when we all heard somebody knocking on the front door.

Sophie held her hands out toward us. "Don't move. Stay here." She poked her head out the door and then pulled it back in. "There's a cop at the door."

"Jackson?" How in the hell did he catch up to me?

But she was shaking her head. "No. A uniform. I'll be right back."

I held the door open after she left and strained to hear the conversation.

I heard the tones of the security pad as she disengaged the alarm, then the keys as she unlocked the door.

"We're closed, officer. Sorry. You'll have to come back tomorrow."

"Everything okay in here?" I didn't recognise the voice. It was deep and the result of years of smoking.

"Why wouldn't it be?"

"You're here by yourself?"

"Of course I am. I've got a lot of work to do. If it's okay with you, I've got to get back to it."

There was a pause. Then, "Okay. Keep the door locked."

"It was locked before you disturbed me, officer."

I heard the door close, the jangle of her keys and the tones of the alarm system. There was a delay of about a minute, and I was seconds from heading out to rescue her when she walked in.

"What took you so long?"

"He was talky."

"No," I said, "after the alarm was set."

She ignored me. "You almost finished there, Alf?"

He pulled the USB cable from the computer. "Almost. I take it we don't want video of us in here tonight?"

Shit. I hadn't thought of that. "Can you do something about that?"

He looked at Sophie. "You have a cleaning crew come through here?"

"Right after closing. They just left."

"Same people every time?"

"No, a company sends whatever crew they can get."

Alf nodded and started typing. "And who's in first in the morning?"

"Usually Terry. He's gunning for Harris' spot. He comes in and gets the terminals fired up and ready for the day."

He finished typing. "Easy. I've just deleted the videos since 5:00 this evening. Unplug the computer from the wall and blame the cleaners. If Terry doesn't pick up on it, find some reason to be in here and make sure there's a report filed."

"The cleaners will get fired, though. I can't do that."

Alf stood from the desk and reached over and unplugged the computer. "No they won't. The company will roster them off to another client for a few months." He slid the hard drive into his pocket. "We should get the hell out of here before I end up in a cell with my client."

"Good idea." I gave Sophie a kiss on the cheek. "I owe you, big time. Let's get out of here."

Sophie led us to the door and held it open after Alf and I were on the sidewalk. "I'm staying, Mac. I've got a feeling you're account isn't the only funny one."

"Nothing funny about it."

She slowly closed the door. "Take care, Mac. I'll see you later. I've got real work to do."

She locked the door and set the alarm, and

disappeared into the bank.

Alf patted me on the back. "I think she likes you, pal."

"Go watch some movies, Alf. I've got some thinking to do."

"Don't hurt yourself."

Chapter Twenty-Two

Alf went on his way, and I slid my hands into my pockets and went on a contemplative walk. Alf would find the video I needed. That box was ticked. I was walking past a patio bar, wondering where I might find Barry and my car, when I saw my ex, Jane, sitting at a table with Terry. I stopped walking and watched for a minute. An upright propane heater stood beside them, but it didn't look like they needed it. The two of them were generating enough heat on their own. Jane had cut her hair. The dark brown curls that used to be well below her shoulder blades were now well above her collar.

Terry had a grin plastered across his face, soaking in whatever was radiating off Jane. Actually, that's not fair. She was something special. Just not for me.

I walked up to the railing from behind Jane and face-on with Terry. "Hey, Terry, marry her, will you? Put me out of my financial misery."

Jane didn't even turn her head to look at me. "Keep walking, Mac, or I'll stab you in the eye with my fork."

I smiled and kept looking at Terry. "You're a brave man, my friend. I'd try to dissuade you, but my financial best interests come first."

Jane lifted the napkin off her lap, threw it on the table and stood. I took a slight step back. She didn't turn my way but addressed Terry. "I need to go to the ladies, Terry. Please promise me you won't talk to this psychotic."

I chuckled. "I'll leave him alone. Go powder your nose."

Her right fist clenched. I was on the highest level of alert. But she took a deep breath, still not looking at me, relaxed her hand and walked around the other diners into the main body of the restaurant.

I waited until she was well out of sight before I spoke. "So, Terry, you and Jane are hitting it off pretty well, by the looks of it."

"You really should go. She seemed pissed off."

"I'm helping you, mate. The more pissed she is at me, the better she'll treat you, being as you're not me. In any way at all."

He thought about that for a minute. I didn't have a minute. "I'm kinda surprised she's going out with you." I pointed at the table and the food and wine. "This is a date, right?"

That got his back up. "Why are you surprised?"

"You're so much younger. You can't be more than thirty."

"I'm forty-three."

"Really? Shit. Same as me. You wear it a lot better. When's your birthday?"

"October twelfth."

"So forty-four in a month. Damn. I look at least ten years older than you." I was. I nodded at him, turned to leave, and then did one of those things Columbo always did. The 'one more thing' turn. "Oh, hey. Have you met my dog yet?"

He shook his head. "Not really. I saw her in the back of Jane's car once. Nice looking Border Collie."

"You saw *him*. That's Lincoln. You a dog person?"

He shrugged and glanced at the restaurant, looking for Jane, I guess. "Allergic. More of a cat person, actually."

I grimaced and sucked air in through my teeth. "Jane's not going to like that. I'm both. Cat and dog. I love them all. I still remember my first cat. A gorgeous Siamese. Rosebud, because she always ate the rose petals off the plants in the garden."

Terry smiled, off in memory land. "Mine was Mittens. A little calico."

I tapped on the rail with my knuckles. "Okay then. I should piss off before she gets back. Don't want to get stabbed. You watch your back, okay?"

"I think you're exaggerating about her. She's not that bad."

"I hope so." I thought about it for a second. "Actually, you're probably right. It's probably me. Never know when to hold the door or shut up around her."

I turned to leave, then turned back for one more bit of information.

"Terry Dempsey, right?"

"My name? Yeah. Why?"

"Is your mum Shirley Dempsey, who babysat for me when I was a little kid? Always smelled like peppermint candy. Probably had them hidden in her pockets."

He was getting really annoyed now. "No. It's Vivian. And she would have still been a Knox back then."

I frowned. "I don't think so. We're the same age, right?" Wrong. "Could have been Dempsey. She has red hair, right?"

"Blonde. Mac, she will be back in a minute, and I don't want you here."

I leaned forward over the rail until I was in his face and spoke quietly. "You're afraid of her."

"Yeah. No. I mean, she's—"

"She's way over the top. Hasn't learned the word 'compromise' yet. Never will. You have a smart head on your shoulders if you're afraid of her. You should be." I pulled back and looked in the restaurant. "And she's not here yet. I bet she's waiting for me to leave before she returns." I turned sideways and rested a butt cheek on the railing. "I could stay here all night."

Terry deflated. His shoulders dropped, and he lowered his head. "Fuck, Mac. Don't do this."

"Oh, relax. I'm leaving. Don't want to screw up your chance for a root." I tapped the railing with my knuckles. "Have a good evening, Terry. And I was serious. Marry her. I'm tired of sending her money."

I didn't listen to whatever it was he said in response. I turned to leave in my quest for Barry and my car. I wasn't two steps toward the TAB, above which sat my apartment slash office, when a police car came to a screeching stop in front of it. Difficult with the ABS systems in most cars, but Jackson figured out a way to do it. He piled out of the car with another detective and sprinted his lard-arse up my stairs.

I was a target. Again. Shit.

Chapter Twenty-Three

"Fuck, fuck, fuck." I launched myself over the restaurant railing and ploughed through the diners. A waiter dropped a tray of salt and pepper calamari behind me. I pushed into the inside of the restaurant and made a beeline for the back.

The kitchen doors were clogged with wait staff. I had too much trouble getting through there. The bathrooms, though, had large windows. I ducked into the first one I got to and literally ran into Jane on her way out. She'd been paying attention in her cardio-boxing class. I ducked just in time to avoid a right cross to the kisser.

"Temper, temper, Jane. Violence never solved anything."

"Asshole. What are you doing in here?"

I continue into the ladies' room and toward the frosted window on the back wall. "Can't stop and chat. People to do, things to see." I tried unfastening the latch at the top of the window. It hadn't been opened in years, by the feel of it. I clenched my jaw, grabbed tighter and wrenched with all of my not inconsiderable strength.

I felt it give a smidge and re-doubled my efforts, trying to ignore the screaming from my ribs.

"Who's chasing you?"

I grunted and freed the latch from its rusty grip. "Whazzat? Jackson. He's probably on his way back down my stairs and in hot pursuit." I pushed up on the top of the frame until it raised enough to get my fingers under the bottom. I hoisted and made a gap large enough to get out. "Don't tell him you've seen me, okay?"

"What have you done now?"

"Not a fucking clue." I lifted a leg through. "But he's busting to get me, so I need to get out of the frame until I figure out what the fuck's going on."

I swung my other leg out and ducked through, dropping the half metre to the parking lot. It was kind of anticlimactic, that short drop.

The window slid shut behind me. Jane was on the ball. At least she seemed to be helping me.

Other than the light filtering out through the frosted glass from the bathroom, the only light in the alley behind the restaurant was from a weak street light at the far end of the block. I looked around. Skips at the far end overflowed with trash from the eatery. In the other direction was the main street and the only source of light. I was alone. I took a step back into a dark corner. If Jackson poked his head down the alley, there was no point in being an easy target.

I slid the prepaid phone out of my back pocket and dialled the only number programmed in it. Six seconds later, I heard a phone ringing, both in my ear and from a real phone somewhere else in the alley.

The ringing stopped, and the call was terminated on my phone.

"That you, Mac? You're a shitty hider. I can see

your feet."

I looked down. The tip of my shoe was out of the shadow, reflecting enough of the weak streetlight to make it stand out like a beacon in the dark. Damn.

I flipped the phone closed and stepped into the light, such as it was. Barry pushed out from between two skips with the other phone in his hand.

I quickly looked down the alley to the road and pulled Barry back out of the light. "I'm well and truly fucked, Baz."

"Lucky you."

My eyes watered, and I shifted position to allow what little breeze there was to come from behind. "Wow, mate. How do you get to that level of smell so fast?"

"Years of practice. What's happening?"

"I need somewhere to lie low for a little while."

Barry laughed. "I'd let you stay at my place," he waved his arms expansively around the trash heaps, "but it's a bit of a mess."

Wrong guy, wrong problem. I closed my eyes and rubbed my forehead with the heel of my hand. "Right. You're absolutely right. Change of subject, then. What did you find out at the beach?" I looked at the time on the phone. "It's only 7:00. Don't you think you should have hung around a bit longer?"

Barry patted his pockets, finally settling on the back left. He pulled out my car keys. "The cops were out there. A bunch of them. And just after they left, a black truck with those rims that spin showed up, and the two guys you described, a shaggy and a chrome dome, got out."

"You see where they went after that?"

"Nah. Hung around for a little while, then headed back here." He handed me the keys. "You need petrol."

"Of course I do. You parked it behind my place?"

"I did. You should know that Jackson came tearing out of your place with someone else, hell-bent for leather looking for you." Barry looked down the alley. "Frothing at the mouth. Almost killed me coming down those stairs."

"Wonder what that asshole wants now."

"I asked," said Barry. "Seemed like the thing an assistant detective would do." He held out his hand.

Palm up.

I dug a couple of twenties out of my pocket and handed them over. "What did he say?"

He snapped the bills between his fingers and folded them neatly into a filthy nylon wallet. The Velcro tear sound echoed down the alley when he opened it. He looked up at me. "Thinks you killed Jimmy. Got him out of the way so you would get called into the bank."

"Figures. The guy's an idiot. He's going to be parked at my place for a while. Until he finally figures out I'm not coming back. I've got to get out of here. You didn't see me, right?"

"See who? I'm an old drunk. My testimony is easily impeached. Get out of here."

Chapter Twenty-Four

I left the stink of the alley and Barry and trotted to the street. I eased my head around the corner and looked for evidence of Jackson or his friends. Except Jackson doesn't have friends.

I turned left around the corner onto the street, and after a couple of steps, Jackson walked around a corner toward me, about half a block away. I took a couple of more steps toward him, on autopilot, before the message got from my brain through to my feet. At about the same time, Jackson yelled and started running at me. Shit. I spun and ran back the way I came. I got around the corner into the alley and stopped—dead end. I pressed against the wall and listened to his flat, sloppy feet pounding closer.

Timing is everything. He careened around the corner, gun in hand, and I pushed off the wall and slammed him sideways, taking advantage of his angular momentum on the corner. He spun, his handgun flying out of his meaty hand and flying past my head. It just missed me and then bounced off the wall behind me. Jackson bellowed some shit in my general direction, and he landed on his ass and bounced his head off the asphalt.

He groaned, and I ran. It took everything I had to resist kicking the fat fuck in the ribs before I went, but I didn't think I could afford the time. I needed to get out of sight and quickly.

I wasn't built for speed anymore, and heavy breathing strained my pain limits, but I hoofed it across the street as fast as I could. Angled to the bank and rapped on the glass door. Sophie was sitting at her desk, headphones on, her back to the door, oblivious to my knocking. I rapped a little harder, and she turned, saw me, removed her headphones and walked to me. Slowly. Really, really slowly. I impatiently waved at her to move faster, taking quick looks over my shoulder.

She cleared the alarm and unlocked the door, pulling it open a crack. "Mac? What's up?"

"I need to get off the streets, like right now."

"In here?"

"Jesus, Soph. Let me in. I'll explain once I'm out of sight."

She frowned and pulled the door open. Not fast enough. I helped with a little shove. I think she took it the wrong way.

"What the hell?"

"Lock up." I ducked into Harris' office and waited for her.

Harris had a half-decent supply of booze. I poured a healthy drop of Tullamore Dew and tossed it back. Poured a second and sat in his chair. A stack of official-looking papers was neatly piled on one corner of the desk. I was thumbing through them when Sophie walked in and closed the door behind her, a little on the firm side.

"I said, what the hell?"

I sipped and sat back in Harris' chair. "Jackson's

on the warpath. I've killed Jimmy, apparently."

"And you're running? You've got to turn yourself in and let the facts speak for themselves."

I stood and took her by the shoulders and kissed her on the forehead. "Oh, Sophie, you innocent. I'm fucked. I need to unravel all of this before Jackhole catches up with me. And I think I'm going to need your help."

She shook her head. "Nothing I can do. You're the detective. I'm just—"

"Not 'just' anything, Soph. The number one rule in cases like this is to follow the money. And who better to help than someone from within the money house?" She was wavering, I could tell. I took her by the hands and gently squeezed them. "I didn't take the money, and I sure as hell didn't kill Jimmy. But if Jackson takes me in, the investigation is over, and whoever is behind this skates."

She squeezed back and sighed. "What could I possibly do?"

"Other than let me hide in here for a little while? Do some digging with me."

"I'm not a detective, Mac."

I pulled Harris' chair back and invited her to sit. "Dig into the bank accounts. Four and a half million is missing. Two fifty in my account. My invisible account. I bet the rest of that four and a half is spread around other invisible accounts." I pointed at the terminal on Harris' desk. "Can you see if you can find them?"

Forty-five minutes later, Sophie pushed herself away from the desk. "Nothing." She held up a hand. "Hints of something, but nothing definite." She stood and stretched. I've got to get out of here. *We've* got to get out of here."

"You could see my account, though, right?"

She nodded and leaned over Harris' computer, clearing her history and logging out. "Like a beacon."

"Shit." I took her by the arm. "Do you have a laptop?"

"Of course I do."

"Grab it, and let's get going." I paused at Harris' door and looked out toward the front door. It was clear. "Where's your car parked?"

"I walk to work. My apartment is just up the

road. We can walk. You'll live. It's not that far."

I was about to tell her but decided it would be more effective if she saw it with her own eyes. "Fine. Grab your laptop, and let's get going."

I waited in Harris' doorway while she closed her laptop and slid it into its carry case. She walked past the door and motioned for me to follow.

"No. The back door. Safer."

She stopped. "It's that bad?"

"Maybe worse. You have the code for the back area?"

Chapter Twenty-Five

She entered the code and led me through the back room. "This is going to be on video, Mac."

"Least of my problems." I pushed open the door to the hallway leading to the loading area. "By the time someone thinks to look at this, I'll either be in the slammer for good or free and clear." I turned left at a junction, and Sophie grabbed me by my arm.

"That goes to a maintenance room. This way." She corrected my path to the back door.

We stepped into the area behind the bank, and I watched the door lock behind us. I looked at the eaves of the buildings around us for cameras. I pulled her against the wall. "You want to head to your place, right?"

"Only a couple of blocks from here. We can regroup and decide what to do next."

"Stick to the shadows and don't cross any streets without checking first. And hold up before we get to your apartment building, okay?"

"What's going on?"

"Hopefully nothing, but better safe than sorry."

We slid along the walls like a bad imitation of some World War II spy movie, ducking across streets like the SS were on our tails.

I pulled up just short of an intersection, leaning against the brick wall of the post office. "You're just ahead, right?"

"Yeah. Why did you stop?"

I leaned my head around the corner. Took a quick look and pulled back. "Jackson is leaning against a police car four buildings down. Look and tell me if it's in front of your apartment building. His car is on the other side of the street."

Sophie stepped past me, looked around the corner and pulled back. "Shit. Directly across. Is he looking for me?"

I pulled her alongside me, our backs against the wall. "I was afraid of that. They're looking for an inside person, and you've pulled the short straw."

"Me?"

I shrugged and pointed my thumb in the direction of her place. "Might just be looking for me. Not worth the risk, though. They're going to pick you up as an accessory for the robbery, and if they've linked us for that, they might try the same for Jimmy's murder. We need to get the hell out of here."

"No way."

I took her gently by the shoulders. "We really need to go. If he's camped out here, I should be able to get my car."

"We should turn ourselves in."

"Soph, hon, someone has set us up. I'm not sure who, but for four and a half million dollars, you know they've got a lot of incentive to bury us. Sorry you got pulled into this mess, but I've got to figure out who did this, or we're both going to jail for a very long time."

I took her by the hand, and we ran back to the

TAB and my car. Not suspicious looking at all.

I paid cash for a cabin at the Wayfarer for the night. I left the car in the main parking lot and walked to the cabin. There was no point in advertising which one we were in.

"How do you know about this place?"

I chuckled. "Some of my clients aren't the classiest. This place comes highly recommended by some of them." I pointed to the end of a string of cabins. "We're in the last one. Made sure there were two beds."

A cabin door opened beside us, and Ernie spilled out, buttoning up his shirt. He stopped walking when he saw me, slowly tucking his shirt into his brown corduroy pants. "Mac. Um, look." He swallowed. I smiled. "Mac, look, are you going to tell Betty? Oh, fuck it." He pulled out his wallet and fed me a pile of twenties. "We're good?"

I fanned the bills, butted the edges together and folded them in half. "We're good." I slid the bills into my pocket. "You're going to hurt yourself if you're not careful."

"Yeah, well. Thanks."

I winked at him and slapped him on the back. "Get the fuck outta here. And if anyone asks, *you* didn't see *us*, okay?"

"Got it. Absolutely." He finished tucking in his shirt and disappeared into the dark.

"Was that Ernie?"

"We saw nothing, right?" I watched as headlights came on, and Ernie drove out of the parking lot. I looked back at the cabin Ernie had come from. The curtains moved slightly, and a light went out behind them.

"Is Ernie messing around on Betty again?"

I cocked an eyebrow and continued walking to our assigned cabin.

"And you're covering his ass, aren't you?"

I didn't answer. I used my phone to shine a light on the door and unlocked it. Then, I flipped on the switch and looked at the small room.

Sophie pushed past me and wrinkled her nose. "Not five-star, that's for damned sure."

I closed the door behind us and latched it with the security chain. A misnomer if there ever was one.

Any kid over the age of twelve could kick through one of those things.

Sophie placed her laptop case on the small desk and sat in the chair, leaning her head back, closing her eyes and stretching her arms. She opened her eyes and looked up at me. "We're doing this tonight, right?"

I unzipped the case and pulled out her laptop. "I am. You can sleep if you want, but it'll be faster with your help."

She groaned and sat up a little straighter. "Together, then. You'll keep me awake anyway."

Chapter Twenty-Six

Sophie left the chair and tested one of the beds with a single index finger. "This place is a rat hole."

"But it's our rat hole." I slid into the chair and opened her laptop. "How do you make this thing work?"

She laughed. "You're a luddite. Move."

I ceded the seat to her and watched as she started the laptop, selected a Wi-Fi channel and VPNed to the bank.

"I don't know what you're expecting, Mac. I couldn't find anything while I was there. What makes you think I'll find something now?"

"Check your account."

She typed a few keystrokes. "Shit. Almost the same as yours." She took out her phone and opened her phone banking app. "And it's not visible here."

"And you can't find any other large changes in balances that took place over the past few weeks?"

She shook her head. "Nothing out of the ordinary. A couple of clubs made large deposits, but they're known to do that every once in a while." She sighed and dropped her hands in her lap. "None of this is making any sense."

I actually thought it was. At least it was starting to. "You've got a way to recover your password when you've forgotten it, haven't you?"

"Every company does. But I haven't forgotten my password." She pointed at the laptop screen. "Obviously."

"Terry's forgotten his."

"What?"

I sat on the edge of the bed. Sophie had to turn in the chair to talk to me. She had a nice profile. "A couple of things have been bothering me. I need a bit more info first, though. Log in like you're Terry, but he forgot his password."

"You lost me."

"Your login account name: First initial and last name? 'spatterson' in your case?"

"Yes." She looked at me, then turned and looked at the laptop. "Terry's would be 'tdempsey' then."

"Try it."

"Why Terry's account?

"He's Assistant Manager and as such will have higher permissions than you do. Try it."

Sophie clacked away at the keyboard for a minute. "Okay, but so what? I don't have his password."

"Do whatever it is you do when you forget a password and need to recover it."

She tapped a couple of keys and shook her head. "Need his birth date."

"October 12th, 1975."

She hesitated for a second, then typed it in. "How in the hell did you know that?"

"I'm a detective. I detect. What next?"

A window popped up on the screen. "It's giving me an option of one of three security questions."

"And they are?"

Sophie activated a pull down window. "Mother's maiden name, name of first pet and street you grew up on."

I smiled. Social hacking was dead easy. "Pick the first pet name. Mittens. Cute little calico cat."

She furrowed her brow, made the entry and sat back. After a brief pause a second window popped up with a link to reset the password. "Son of a bitch."

"Okay. Get back in there and see what you can find out."

Sophie turned in her chair and looked at me through squinted eyes. "How long have you known Terry?"

"Not that long, actually. A couple of years."

"I've known him for seven. Wouldn't have been able to tell you any of his info."

I made a circular motion with my finger. "Turn around, Sophie. Dump all the deposits for the past three months and log off as fast as you can. I'm pretty sure Jackson is looking for you just as hard as he's looking for me."

"But—"

I sat forward. "I know *some* things about computers. Your laptop has a unique hardware address. Somewhere, it will be logged that *your* computer logged in with Terry's credentials. Best not stay on too long. They'll track the IP to this place pretty quickly."

She looked at me for another couple of seconds, realisation dawning in her gorgeous chocolate brown eyes. "Oh, you asshole."

"I've been called that a lot, lately."

"You've set *me* up."

I scooted forward, placed my hands on her shoulders and gently turned her back to the screen. "You were set up a long time ago. I'm helping you—us—get un-set up. Dump it all and disconnect."

Her fingers flew across the keys. Download bars crept from 0% to 100% with agonising slowness. After no more than five minutes, she disconnected the Wi-Fi connection and sat back in her chair. "Everything is on my drive. Every account in the branch. I didn't know Terry had that kind of access. I thought only Harris did." She took a deep breath and frowned. "So I need to find suspiciously large balances in accounts that are normally not that flush."

I pulled a chair up beside her. "Exactly."

"Have you figured this out yet?"

I shook my head. "Not yet. Not all the way. Yet." I looked at the time on my phone. "It's getting late. How fast can you do this?"

She opened the file using a spreadsheet program. "Fast. I can pivot the data on account names and look at balances three months ago compared to today. Our fat accounts didn't even exist three months ago, so that's the first filter—new accounts. The second filter is new accounts with balances substantially higher than other existing accounts."

She typed as she talked and stopped as a list of fifteen names resolved on the screen. "What's your ex-'s name?"

"Jane."

"Last name?"

"Golding."

Sophie pointed at the screen. "You think an intern would have this kind of money in her account?"

The balance was similar to Sophie's and mine.

"Fourteen have the same balance, roughly."

Sophie nodded. "Both of us, Jane, and eleven others. A total of three and a half million dollars."

"There's a million short."

She pointed to the last name on the list. "New account. No other account, in the name of David Thomson, with a balance of one million."

I rubbed my eyes with the heels of my hands. I felt like half of Budgewoi Beach was lodged in my eyes. "I'm missing something. Someone steals all that money and distributes it evenly among fifteen unsuspecting people? To what end?"

"I've got to log back in again." Sophie reconnected the Wi-Fi, signed into the VPN and logged in as Terry again.

"Risky. What are you looking for? What have I missed?"

"I don't think you've missed anything." She opened three windows: one with her accounts, one with mine and one with Jane's. "You really shouldn't be looking at Jane's information, Mac. It's confidential. Don't tell anyone, okay?"

I barked out a laugh. "Yeah. Mum's the word."

She pointed at the three windows. "It doesn't make sense, does it, to spread that money around with no way to access it?"

"That's what's bugging me."

She clicked a link on all three windows. "There's a second signatory on the new accounts. Has rights to withdraw or transfer the entire amount." She pointed at the name on all three windows. "Garry Goresh. On all of the accounts, including David Thomson's."

"So we find this Goresh guy, and it's all over."

Sophie closed her laptop and slid it back into its case. "I've lived here my entire life. I've never heard of a Goresh. And no David Thomson's either. Billy and Joey Thomson, but no David. So what now?"

I heard sirens in the distance, getting louder. Sophie heard them, too. I could tell by the look of 'oh shit' on her face. "We need to get our asses out of here."

I pulled an envelope and pencil out of the desk drawer, wrote on it and left it in the centre of the bed. The sirens were closer. "Let's get out of here."

Chapter Twenty-Seven

A large sedan with flashing blue and red lights in the grill pulled into the far end of the parking lot just as Sophie and I left the cabin. I grabbed her by the arm and ran between the cabins to the parking lot, staying in the shadows. We reached the main office just as Jackson did. I held out my arm and kept Sophie from running around the corner. We watched Jackson barrel into the Wayfarer office with a colleague in tow.

We stopped under a window and listened to Jackson make an ass of himself.

"We know they're here. Look at these pictures.

What cabin are they in?" Jackson was in full bellow. Influencing people and making new friends, like always.

The clerk behind the counter must have pointed at a map because I didn't hear him say anything before Jackson barrelled back out. He barrels a lot. Makes sense since he looks a lot like one.

We were in my car before he hit the cabin's front door, and we were on the street before he found my note on the bed.

"Close." Sophie craned her neck and watched the Wayfarer recede.

I took back roads to her apartment. "Thanks to you, I've got enough to finish this, I think. You need to leave town for a couple of days. Don't want you caught in the crossfire."

"Bullshit, Mac. I'm not running from anyone."

I pulled to the curb just around the corner from her apartment building. "You're in Jackson's sights, and you'd be smart to get out of his range while I finish him off."

"Finish him—you're going to kill him?"

"Oh, Jesus, no. I've got to talk to Harris and

expose him for what he is. He's either the guy on the inside or knows who it is. You wouldn't happen to know his address, do you?"

She opened her laptop. "It'll be in his account information." She typed a few commands and texted me the address. I pulled to a stop, and she looked out the windscreen. "You've taken me home? Go around the corner and park out front."

"Might still be an audience." I opened the door and put a foot out. "If it's clear, pack a bag and get out of here. You have any family around here?"

"Sister in Newcastle. I can go up there."

I got back in the car. "No they'll look there. Head to Gosford. Take the train. Don't use your Opal card. Buy a ticket. Use cash. Stay in a lower-scale motel. Turn your phone off, too. I'll find you when it's all finished here."

"How?"

"I'm a detective. It's what I do." I got out of the car. "Wait until I check if it's clear."

I eased my head around the corner and looked at the empty street. I motioned for her to follow and walked her into her apartment. I waited while she packed a bag. On the way back to the car, I took three hundred of Helen's money and pressed it into her hands. "Take this. Don't use an ATM."

She looked at me like she was finally taking this seriously, pale under the streetlights. I held the door for her and then got in the driver's side. "I'll take you to the station in Morisset." I looked at the time on my phone. "There'll be a train in twenty minutes."

"And what are you going to do while I'm gone?"

"Finish this."

We drove in silence for the ten minutes it took to get to the station. I pulled into the 'kiss-and-go' spot, reached across her and opened her door. "Thanks very much for your help. I couldn't have done this without you. If it all goes pear-shaped, get way out of town for a while. Perth, maybe. I'll make sure everyone knows you had nothing to do with this."

She put the laptop case strap over her shoulder. "Mac, I'd imagined our first night in a hotel a little differently than this."

I smiled. "I want a do-over."

"Deal."

She got out and walked up the stairs to the

pedestrian bridge to the opposite platform. I watched her buy a ticket and sit on the bench. She'd be okay. I had shit to clean up, and I'd do a better job if I weren't worrying about her.

Chapter Twenty-Eight

I wasn't even out of the parking spot when my phone rang. The pre-pay. Baz. "What's up, buddy?"

"Mac?"

"It is. What can I do you for?" I tucked the phone between my neck and shoulder and pulled a hard right across traffic. "You see the truck?"

"Yeah. Those shaggies are at that burger place. You know the one. Puts the fuckin' pineapple on their burgers."

I knew the place. Didn't frequent it much. Pineapples on a burger are beyond the pale. "You're there now? You can see them?"

"Through the front window. It's like they're hitting on one of the ladies in there. On the turps, by the looks of it. Shouldn't really be driving."

"You're one to talk."

"I walked here." He sounded a little pissed off.

"Relax, mate. I'm heading over. Hang around." I hung up, pulled a marginally legal U-turn and headed west. I needed to see these guys and find out if they were the twats who put a beating on me. And then get them out of the picture. From the train station to the pineapple burger place took me near the police station. I needed the police for this, but not Jackson, and not in person.

I thumbed in the station's number as I drove, taking the long way around, staying on the small streets and out of traffic.

"NSW Police. How may I help you?"

I threw on the most bogan accent I could manage. "Ya know that bloke what robbed the bank? I seen him just now."

"Can I get your name, sir?"

Not likely. "He's at that pineapple burger place just down from the dog track. Looked like he had a gun." I hung up and came at the burger joint from the back. I parked beside a pile of garbage bags and eased myself around the front. I could see Baz sitting on the sidewalk across the road, back against a storefront, keeping an ever-vigilant eye on the front of the place. And virtually invisible to the world.

I took a quick scan of the street. No obvious police. Yet. I had a couple of minutes at most. I came around the corner and through the front door. I heard Baz call out my name as the door swung shut behind me. I grimaced. I hope he kept it down. I didn't need any advertising.

The two surfers were easy to spot. It would have been easy to spot with my eyes closed. They were in desperate need of a shower. Baldy and Shaggy sat across from and diagonal to each other at a table for four. A waitress stood at the side of the table, order pad in her hand and a look of impatience on her face.

I quickly slid into the seat beside Baldy, directly across from Shaggy. "Boys. Fancy running into you here." I looked up at the waitress. "Have they been bothering you, ma'am?"

"Nothing I can't handle."

"Well, you don't have to worry much longer. The police are on their way."

Baldy had shifted sideways in his chair by this time and poked me in the chest. "What the fuck?"

I looked at him, then across at Shaggy. "That hurt. You guys pack a mean punch." I rubbed my ribs. "And the cops have enough evidence to put you away for beating poor Jimmy to death." A little bullshit never hurt anybody.

Sirens grew louder. I had maybe thirty seconds. "Do you hear sirens? Or am I getting paranoid, boys?" I smiled at Shaggy. "You're going to make someone a nice girlfriend behind bars."

Shaggy took the knife off the table and dove for the waitress, grabbing her around the neck. "Fucking hell, man. I thought we were hooked up. Fucking cop."

Shit. I didn't expect this. I stood, hands out, attempting some level of placating him. "Don't make it worse, mate." Baldy backed up fast, tipping the chair and heading for the kitchen and the inevitable back way out. I swung a leg out and tripped him, his forehead bouncing off the table at the booth next to him. He dropped like a sack of rice.

A squad car, lights and siren making their presence known landed in front of the burger joint. Shaggy's concentration broke for a second, and I drove my heel into the side of his knee. He dropped to the floor, the knife skittering away. I toe-punted him in the ribs and looked toward the kitchen and my escape. The waitress was backing away, shocked. I took her hand and stopped her. "Let the cops know what happened." I looked out of the window at a couple of uniforms getting out of the squad car. "I've got to run."

I ducked through the kitchen door and dodged a man in a white apron with a sharp knife. "Playing through." I hit the back door and deposited myself beside my car. Handy. But I had to see what happened to the two arseholes.

I eased to the front again, poking my head around the corner of the building. A second squad car had shown up. I watched for almost a minute before Baldy and Shaggy were escorted out of the restaurant in cuffs. Shaggy was yelling up a storm, and Jackson's name was used frequently. Baldy looked stunned. He was probably concussed. I smiled. Or maybe not. He's got a pretty hard head.

I waited until both cars had left before I crossed the road and sat beside Baz. "Good job, mate. That's them out of our hair."

"What was that about?"

I patted him on the arm. "You recognised them through that booze haze?"

"Haven't had a drink in days, Mac. Cops got 'em. That's good, right?"

"Got them on a pretty minor thing, I'm afraid, but maybe," I paused.

"Maybe what?"

I thought about it for a second. "I think I got Shaggy worried enough about Jimmy's beating that he'll roll on Baldy. He was the weaker of the two. I saw it often enough when I was a cop. He'll jump at the chance to take the lighter sentence." I shrugged. "Let's see how it goes. They're off the streets for now."

I pushed myself to my feet. "Now I've got to find Harris." I looked at the address on my phone. "I wonder what his bedtime is?"

Chapter Twenty-Nine

Harris had to be the man inside. It was a process of elimination. Terry was too slow, Sophie was as framed up as I was, and nobody else had access. Getting him to admit it, though, without any of the official persuasive techniques I could use as a copper, would be tricky.

According to the personal information attached to the bank account, Harris lived in a ground-floor apartment in a nice part of town. Of course. Security would probably be tight but electronic. There would be no need for personal security for a bank manager, even if he were worth four and a half mill. Or would be.

I parked half a block away from his apartment building. Still had no idea how I was going to get to him. I was the last guy he would want to see. At night. Alone.

It's not like I know how to pick locks. That's TV bullshit. As a cop, I had a couple of big guys with a ram who could take down any door I encountered. Not subtle. And the boys were not currently available.

I stood outside the building in the middle of the walkway. The short walk had provided no inspiration. I doubted a random buzzer push, pretending to be a pizza delivery guy, would get the main door open. And even if it did, there was still his apartment door to get through. I rested my hand on the butt of my weapon. Shooting my way in wasn't an option, either.

"Excuse me."

Someone brushed past me on the way in. I recognised the fat neck from behind. And the expensive but ill-fitting suit. I'll take luck over skill any day.

I ghosted in behind him and entered the common area before he noticed. By then, my handgun was out.

"Durridge. What the fuck are you doing here? The cops are looking for you."

He reached into his inside suit pocket, and I raised my revolver, pointing it at his chest. "Hey, Harris. Stop that." I gestured with the barrel. "Into your apartment."

"You going to kill me like you killed Jimmy?"

I shook my head and gave him a shove with my free hand. "Nice try. Open your door."

He fumbled with his keys and opened the door. I pushed him through, closed the door behind us, and jabbed him in the back with the gun. "Make yourself comfortable. We've got some talking to do."

"Fuck you, Mac." Harris dropped into a chair by his small fireplace. Photos of Harris and friends at the beach, on the ski hills and on the tail end of a yacht filled the mantle.

"Fuck me? Fuck me? You've already fucked me." I smiled. "I'm off the hook for Jimmy, though. Baldy and Shaggy were picked up less than an hour ago. Baldy's going to roll. I'd bet my life on it. You didn't even get a text from Jimmy, did you? Easy enough for the cops to check your phone records.

"That just leaves the money. I'm still trying to figure out how you're doing this. I got most of it figured out, but I haven't completely figured out how you pulled the moneybag switch. Almost, but not completely. I saw the note about the upcoming audit on your desk. That must have loosened your stools."

"What the fuck do you care?"

I laughed. "Stupid questions for $100, Alex." I wiggled the barrel at him. "Get up. We're going to the bank, and you're going to walk me through it."

"Fuck you."

"I'm starting to think you may have feelings for me, Harris." I pressed the muzzle into the meat of his thigh. "It'll be noisy, but I'll be gone before the cops arrive. And you'll never walk right again." I pointed at the photos. "Or ski." I pressed harder. "Get the fuck up."

I took a step back and waited for him to stand. He hesitated, then pushed himself up. "My car is parked downstairs. I'll have it brought around."

"Oh, fuck off. I'm driving. You'll have to put up with a twenty-year-old Corolla and all of its smells." I gestured to the door. "Walk, and make no stupid noises. You piss me off, and I'll kneecap you. I'm tired and losing what sense of humour I have left."

Harris grunted and gave me a wide berth. "Fuck. Relax." I grabbed the back of his suit jacket in a bunch and jabbed the muzzle into his spine.

He looked over his shoulder. "Take it easy. That hurt."

"Do anything stupid, and you'll be pushing yourself around in a wheelchair for the rest of your miserable life."

Harris walked out of his apartment, and building, with me in tight formation. No surprises, no unnecessary noises, marched in lockstep like a good little soldier. I eased up a bit once we were out of the building and pushed him toward the car.

He slowed as we got closer. "That? Really?" He jabbed his thumb over his shoulder. "We seriously can take the Merc. I'll behave."

"What was that you said before? Oh yeah. Fuck you. Get in the car."

I held the gun on him while he got in and kept it trained on him as I got in the driver's seat. I pointed it across my body at him. "One twitch, Harris, and I'll do something we'll both regret."

Chapter Thirty

I parked at a meter in front of the bank. It was extremely unlikely a Parking Ranger would be by at this time of night. I'd be okay for the time I needed to be here.

I reversed the process, getting out and keeping the gun trained on Harris while I walked around to the passenger side of the car. "Out." I stood back from the door. No point getting this far and getting smashed in the knees by the door. Harris levered his fat arse out, and the springs recovered, the car finally levelling.

"You've got to lose a few, Harris." I looked

around. Didn't need an audience for this. "Unlock the door and get us off the street."

Harris looked at me for a second, then dug his keys out of his suit pocket. He bent and released the lock at the base of the door, then the one at chest level. I followed him in. He walked past the alarm panel and into his office.

"No, Harris. The alarm." I pointed at the panel on the wall with my gun. "Before it times out."

He looked at the gun. "You start shooting that thing, and you'll be surrounded by cops before you know what hit you."

"Doesn't worry me. The fucking alarm, Harris."
He sighed. "Fuck you, Mac."
"Broken record." I closed my eyes for a second in thought. I heard a shuffle of feet and opened them, raising the gun at the same time. Stopped him in his fucking tracks.

I trained the gun on Harris while I entered the code I remembered Sophie entering. "Stay put, lard arse." I hit the final digit of the code, and the light turned green. "Okay. Into your office."

He deflated a bit. He looked a lot like the

Michelin Man, just with a little leak. He walked into his office and sat at his desk. I sat in a chair across from him and placed my gun on the desk. "So explain it to me."

"I have no idea what you're talking about. And let me tell you, when all this is over, you'll spend a long time in a cell."

I cocked my head and picked up the gun. Pointed it at his fat head. "Really? 'Garry Goresh'? If you hadn't done that, I'd still be trying to figure out what the hell was going on."

"I'm not following."

"Oh, horseshit. Change the 'y' in Garry to 'ie' and it's an anagram for George Harris. Those kinds of coincidences don't happen. Too clever by half."

"You've been smoking crack."

"You're an idiot. Habib's got these new-fangled digital security cameras. Catches your thugs breaking into my place. Clear as day. Digital zoom, and you can see your five-o'clock shadow." A little bluffing never hurt anyone, right?

Harris stood and walked to his wet bar, uncorking one of the bottles of scotch. He poured a shot and threw it back.

"Let's go, Harris. Back room. I need to walk through this. For my own satisfaction, if you don't mind."

Harris picked up the bottle again, looked at it and threw it at my head. A weak throw, not on target at all. Not even Triple-A material. I ducked and turned to watch it smash against the far wall. "What a waste. That was good stuff." I pointed the gun at him. "Walk."

Harris scrambled for the door, an attempt to escape, I think. I grabbed him by his suit collar and tapped on the side of the head with the butt of the revolver. He grabbed his head and turned on me. I jabbed the barrel into his solar plexus, doubling him over. I placed the barrel under his chin and lifted his head. "The back room. Now."

He hesitated.

"I'm in a shitty mood. Try that again, and you'll have broken ribs to show for it. To the room where we counted."

I followed him to the back room and closed the door behind us.

"You don't know what you're talking about."

I sat on the edge of the table the bill counting machines had been placed and pointed the gun to the floor. "Give me a break, Harris. I was a cop for thirty years, and I've been a private detective for the last five. I've made a living out of figuring things out. And I'm ninety-eight per cent of the way there. I won't be happy until I get that last two per cent. Walk me through it."

Harris stood there, not moving, hands in his pockets.

"Nothing? Really? I should just shoot you now."

"And that would get you nowhere."

"I'd feel better." I looked up at the security camera in the corner of the room. "So we loaded the bags in here. I was left alone for about ten or fifteen minutes with the money, and that, in its entirety, is the case against me."

"Well, that and your word against the bank's. And all that money in your account."

"I didn't mention any money in my account, but let's put that to one side for a moment. You sit there and shut up. I wasn't finished. Where was I? When the truck shows up, I head out through the walkway to the back door and hold the door open. Terry is right behind me. You wheel the trolley full of bags out, and somewhere between this room and the back door, you pulled a switch."

Harris shook his head and smiled at me like I was a simple-headed oaf. "We signed off on the log sheets every step of the way." He picked up the clipboard and waved it in my face. Cocky little shit, and me with a gun.

I took the clipboard and looked at the list of bag serial numbers on it. The numbers swam for a second. I'm not great with numbers, and it had been a long day, but I remembered something Terry did that night and double-checked the list. I smiled, ripped the top page off, and stuffed it in my pocket.

"Harris, you're not as smart as you think you are. You've just given me the piece of the puzzle I couldn't figure out." I waved the gun at him. "Now, walk me through the steps you took to get to the back door."

"That's not going to prove anything."

"I went through the hallway with Sophie earlier

tonight. I think it will prove exactly what I need it to prove. I just need your confirmation."

"Fuck you."

"Jesus, you're boring. Come up with some better repartee." I jabbed him in the ribs. "March."

He winced and pulled away, then opened the door and led me down the hallway. He came to the fork and turned left.

"Hang on. The other way. The heads to the maintenance room." I walked up behind him and placed a hand on his shoulder to turn him around and he sucker punched me. He spun his elbow around and knocked me a lucky shot to the jaw. My gun clattered onto the floor and into Harris' reach. He grabbed it and tried to pull off a snapshot. "No cameras down here, fucknuts."

He was partially successful. The shot punctured my triceps. It missed the bone and any major artery pipes, but it hurt like a son of a bitch. I swept his feet out from under him and grabbed the gun.

"Give me that, fucknuts." I held my hand over the seeping wound and tried to keep the gun level on Harris. "Now look what you've done."

Harris struggled to his feet. "Shoulda killed you."

I took my phone out of my pocket and turned off the recorder. Harris watched and laughed. "You think that's going to do you any good? It'll disappear in the evidence locker."

I placed the muzzle against his forehead and pressed hard. I looked at the panic in his eyes, winked, turned and beat it out the back door.

Chapter Thirty-One

I was leaking. Not profusely. I wouldn't die from it, but I was making a hell of a mess. I stowed my gun, ran around the corner of the bank, and bumped into a sitting Baz.

"How in the hell did you get here so fast?"

"I'm a man of the streets." He slid his back up the wall and stood, squinting. "You're bleeding."

"Don't I know it." I fumbled my car keys out of my pocket and handed them to him.

"You want me to go to the beach again?"

"No. Head north. Leave now. Get up to Newcastle and hang out up there. Leave the car on the street." I pressed a couple of bucks into his hand. "Hop to it, okay? If the cops pull you over, you have no idea where you got the car. You just found it somewhere with the keys in it."

"What's the point?" He looked at the keys in one hand and the money in the other. "What'll you use?"

"Don't worry about me. You're my decoy. I need the cops to think I'm out of town. In the worst-case scenario, you get a couple of days in a warm bed with three squares a day. Are you clear on what I'm asking you?"

"I think so."

"Don't break it. It's the only one I have."

He nodded and wandered off in the general direction of my apartment and the car. I waited until he was out of sight and followed him. I took the prepay out of my pocket and called the police. "Hey, that bank robber guy? I just saw him heading north on the Pacific Highway in his car. Making good time, too."

I hung up and pressed a few more numbers as I headed up the stairs. "Jane. Can you come to my place? I need your help. Medical help. It's an emergency."

I heard a groan at the far end. "It's late."

"Sorry. Did I interrupt you and Terry?"

"Fuck you, Mac."

"I'm getting a lot of that tonight. Seriously, if I've ever meant anything to you in the past, please come over as fast as you can." I hung up and unlocked the door.

I grabbed an old tea towel, wrapped it around my arm and poured a healthy helping of amber pain relief. It lasted three seconds in the glass. I poured a second and had it halfway to my mouth when Jane barged it without knocking. I jumped. Half the scotch landed on my shirt and the rest on the floor.

"Jesus Christ. Nobody fucking knocks anymore."

"What's the emergency?" She put a large, paramedic-quality first-aid box down on my table.

I poured another glass and pointed at the blood on my arm.

"The cops are chasing you, you've been injured—"

"Shot."

"Fantastic. And you think hiding out in your

apartment is a smart thing to do?"

"Last place they'll look." I put down what was left of my drink, took the tea towel off my arm and eased off my shirt.

Jane took a step closer and examined the bruises. "Ouch."

"That's not why I called you. Thanks for coming, by the way." I turned and showed her my arm. "This. Harris shot me."

"Bank guy Harris?"

I nodded and took another sip of scotch. "We had a disagreement over long-term interest rates."

She was good, I've got to give her that. She took one of the few remaining clean towels, soaked it in hot water and gently cleaned the blood off my arm.

I tried to look at the back of my arm at the wound with limited success. Every time I tried to move it, she grabbed me tighter by the wrist, manipulating my arm to the position that best suited her.

She sat back at the table and opened the medical kit. "Harris has a gun? I don't know what surprises me more, that he has a gun or that he missed when he shot you."

"It was my gun." I shook my head. "Don't say it. And he didn't miss. That blood-soaked tea towel is evidence of that."

She took a critical look at the wound once it was cleaned up. "This is nothing."

"Hurts like a son of a bitch."

"What a man. A plaster will fix you. No stitches. Just a little bit of antiseptic and bandage. You'll be pleasuring yourself with that hand in no time."

"For something that's nothing, it sure leaked a fuck of a lot of blood."

She tore off a strip of tape and used it to hold a small piece of gauze in place—a surprisingly small piece of gauze. "You're way too soft. I had Davey in this morning. Tom's son. Not even five. Broke his arm in the playground this morning. Didn't shed a tear when I plastered him up. Makes you look like a little pansy."

It slipped right past me. I poured another glass and took a swig of scotch. It burned my throat before it clicked. "Hang on, what was that?"

"Davey broke his arm. Why?"

Oh, shit. "Nothing. I need to go. I know who got the million, and I've got to reach Sophie before he does, or she's dead. Thanks, Jane. Get out of here. Pretend you didn't hear from me tonight."

I stood and helped her pack up her medical kit and walked her to the door. "Thanks again. Go home."

I was half out the door behind her when I remembered my real phone. I retrieved it from my desk and slid it into the opposite back pocket from the pre-pay. I needed to find Sophie. I should have left her with a phone.

Chapter Thirty-Two

I stood at the bottom of the stairs and flexed my triceps, lightly, to test the bandage and the effect of the liquid painkillers. I'd live.

As it usually happens, what seemed like a good idea thirty minutes ago was turning out to be a bad idea now. I needed my car. I needed any car. And I needed to find Sophie. And I needed to find her before Jackson did.

I called her mobile. It went straight to voicemail like it should have if she had turned the phone off as I asked her to. Dammit. Well, if I couldn't protect Sophie from Jackson, I'd keep Jackson busy until I figured out how to reach her.

A little bit of Tom and Jerry. I'd be Jerry. Jerry always won.

I backtracked to the station on foot, considering options for wheels. I nearly called Baz twice to get him to turn around, but I needed him to pull the trail north for me. From my place to the station was three longish blocks. Jess' parent's cafe was on one of them, Habib's kebab shop on the next, and, just before the station, was a place called, euphemistically, a VIP club. Shitty house music, almost naked dancers and little private areas where more intimate discussions could be had with the talent.

The bass-heavy beat seeped through the cracks as I walked by, then was amplified to almost painful levels as the door opened and my saviour stepped out.

Ernie had one eye closed, trying to focus on the time on his phone, and almost ran into me. His car keys dangled from his left hand. I put an arm out and stopped him from toppling. He wobbled and looked up at me. "Hey, Mac. You going' in? Ask for Amber. She's a little older than the rest, but man, she's shpectacular."

I gently took his keys. "Ernie, my friend, you are way too looped to drive. I'll take your keys. Grab a taxi. I'll get the keys back to you tomorrow."

A puzzled look passed over his face for a second, then a big smile. "Mac, you're a true friend. Just bring them by the house tomorrow, okay?" He placed an index finger against his lips. "Don't tell Betty I was in there, okay?"

He weaved down the sidewalk. I was running out of justifications for covering his ass, but we went way, way back, and I still owed him. A little bit, anyway. I stood in the VIP Lounge parking lot and pressed the 'unlock' button on his key fob. The park lights flashed twice on a blue Mazda 3—nice looking car.

I locked it and left it there. The station was just across the street.

I entered the front door and stepped past the gate that stopped civilians. Walk like you belong. That's the key to getting into places you shouldn't be. A little more difficult in places like police stations and military bases, but I'd been a cop, and most of the people here recognised me and probably thought I was still part of the organisation in one way or another.

The plan, such as it was, involved letting Jackson catch sight of me and then keeping him busy until I thought Sophie was clear. Stupid plan, but it's all I had.

Round support pillars were spaced out across the floor, like sparsely planted trees. One blocked my view of Jackson's desk. I kept it that way until I was up against it. I looked around the side of it, and my plan changed. Jackson had his back to me and was talking with Baldy and Shaggy.

It was a shit plan anyway.

I picked a file folder off a desk next to me and pretended to read it while eavesdropping on the conversation. It didn't sound much like an interrogation.

Jackson almost sounded defeated. "Fuck, guys," he said. "I don't have a choice now. Why'd you grab the knife?"

"I—"

"It was rhetorical. Shut your fucking mouth."

His desk phone rang. "Jackson speaking."

There was a pause while he listened. Then, "Harris, calm down. As soon as I finish with these guys, I'll grab Durridge. Just relax, okay?"

He slammed the phone into its cradle and looked at the two across from him. "Jesus, boys. I need you on the street solving problems, not in here causing more. Come with me. We'll sort this out later."

I watched him remove their handcuffs and motion for them to follow him. I ghosted around the pillar as he walked by, the surf dudes in tow.

I dropped the file folder on a desk and kept a few steps behind them. They walked out of the office, and Jackson turned left. They walked past the black truck and got into Jackson's unmarked car. Both of the surfers sat in the back. I trotted across the street and hopped into Ernie's car. I started it, and Tupac's 'God Bless the Dead' powered out of the speakers. I fumbled with the knobs until I found the volume and lowered it. A lot. Damn. I *really* didn't know.

I pulled out of the parking lot and scanned the road. Taillights disappeared around the corner a couple of blocks ahead, toward the beach. I floored it.

What the fuck was Jackson up to?

Chapter Thirty-Three

I kept a city block between us—or the equivalent. I could have passed them and reached the destination ahead of them, but they were driving so slowly. And it was obvious early on where they were headed.

It was almost half an hour before Jackson pulled into the parking lot near where Jimmy's body was found. I turned off the headlights and coasted down the road, the asphalt lit by the almost full moon.

I rolled to a stop by the side of the road, hard onto the shoulder behind some low-growth shrubbery. I could hear voices when I got out of the car, but I couldn't make out what they were saying.

I tried walking quietly through the parking lot, but there was too much gravel. The crunch sounded like a large herd of bull elephants crashing through a quarry. It didn't matter. By this point they were yelling at each other and not paying much attention to anything else.

There wasn't enough light for a video, so I turned on the voice recorder on my smartphone and inched closer.

Jackson was the loudest. "Boys, why is Mac still alive?"

I peered around a tree. This just got really interesting. Baldy opened his mouth to answer, and Jackson interrupted.

"Shut the fuck up."

"Another body would have been too much attention, Tom."

I moved forward and hid beside a large playground structure. It still smelled faintly of kiddie urine. Jackson pointed to a rock shelf overlooking the surf.

Jackson stood in front of the two, hands on his hips, shaking his head like a headmaster scolding students. "Another body only garners attention if the body is *found*. Make sure it is never found, like you should have done with Jimmy. Jesus, you guys aren't worth the spit in my mouth." He punctuated that with a spit, then walked up to the top of a rock shelf popular with local fishermen. "You take him up here, put a bullet in the back of his head and drop him in the water." He pointed at the foam. "He'd be halfway to New Zealand before sunrise."

"You never said nothing about throwing him off a cliff." Baldy was starting to look a little pissed off.

"I expected you to think for yourself, fucktards. Besides, it's hardly a cliff. It can't be more than three or four metres. Have a look."

I craned my neck to get a better look at them. Jackson waved the surfer dudes up to the shelf. "Look. Perfect spot."

Shaggy and Baldy followed him up to the rock ledge. They stood side-by-side and inched forward, looking down at the rocks below. Jackson took a step back and slid in behind them. He leaned down and pulled a small handgun from an ankle holster. Shit. He took another step back and fired two fast shots, one into the back of each of their heads. Like he told them to do to me. They both dropped like puppets whose strings had been cut.

Jackson threw the gun into the ocean, then grunted as he rolled them both off the ledge and into the water. "See? Much easier this way." He brushed his hands off on his pants. "Idiots."

I dropped to a sitting position beside the playground slide. Son of a bitch. He was insane. I peered around the corner of the playground set and watched as he stood on the shelf, hands on his hips in some stupid power pose, looking out over the water. He took out his phone and scrolled through his contacts. I strained to hear his side of the conversation.

"Lewis? Jackson here. I need you to keep an eye out for someone." He listened for a moment, then interjected. "You're a fucking transit cop. Not a real cop. Shut the fuck up and stop interrupting. You put the word out to keep an eye out for a woman named Sophie Patterson. About 165 centimetres, 70 kilos, late thirties, dark, almost black hair, I don't know, about shoulder length. Do not apprehend her. Call me as soon as she's seen. She'll probably be travelling with that asshole Durridge. Malcolm. Goes by Mac. Early fifties, about 183 cm and at least a hundred kilos. A greasy fat fuck."

That hurt, coming from him. What an arsehole.

He paced the top of the rock flats, listening. "No, me directly. You've got my number." Pause. "No, I don't have pictures of either of them." Another pause. He stopped walking and looked out over the ocean. "It's none of your business what it's about. Just call me when either one of them is found. Immediately when you see either one of them."

He cleared his throat and spat something large enough to be a life form into the ocean. "No, I don't have any intelligence that they are actually on the train. But his car was picked up north of here, so I'm assuming he's not walking out of town. The 'north' part of the story seems to imply they're going the other way."

He hung up and slid the phone into his pocket. "You're both going for a night swim." He turned and walked back toward the parking lot, passing by my location close enough I could smell his body odour. I had to stifle a gag. The guy was rank.

I resisted the urge to trip him as he walked by, jumping on him and beating the shit out of him. I'd probably lose. Even without the fucked up ribs, I'd probably lose. I had other skills. Pugilism wasn't in my portfolio, at least not unless I needed it to be. And even then, only someone smaller and weaker than me.

I should have shot him.

Chapter Thirty-Four

I watched Jackson pull out of the parking lot. I might lose *mano-a-mano*, but I could outsmart the arsehole with one brain cell tied behind my back. Or whatever. I walked back to the street and Ernie's car, deep in thought. I needed help. I made another call I didn't want to make.

I got in the car as the call was picked up on the other end. "Jane, I need your help."

"You get shot again? Is it fatal?"

What a sweetheart. "Nothing like that."

"Then piss off." I could hear Terry in the background asking her who was on the phone. Her reply was muffled. "It's Mac. Don't stop what you're doing. I'll be finished in a sec." Then back to me. "I'm busy. And there's nothing you can tell me that would convince me to help you."

"Wait. Don't hang up." I paused. "Going well with Terry?"

"Fuck off, Mac."

"Okay, okay. Maybe Terry can help, too. I need to track down Sophie."

She snorted derisively. I hate it when she does that. "Nope. Not happening."

"I have to find her before Jackson kills her."

There was an extended silence on the phone. I waited. She felt about Jackson pretty much the same way I did. "Why?"

I assumed that the question referred to the killing and not the finding. "She's stumbled on a bit of fraud. Theft. Over four million worth. You're tied up in the mess, too. Help me find her."

"You need to explain this a bit better." She paused, but before I could stick a word in, she said, "What do you want me to do?"

"She took the train to Gosford. I'm going to

drive down there. I want you to hang out at the Morisset Station in case she backtracks. Call me if she shows up, and keep her under cover. Okay?"

There was another pause. "How am I involved?"

"I'll tell you later. No time right now. I'm heading for Gosford. Please tell me you'll keep an eye on this end."

"Yeah, yeah. Go."

Something finally going my way. "Thanks, Jane. You have no idea how much I appreciate this." I hung up and started the car and made my way toward the highway. Fingers crossed, the cops were busy somewhere else tonight. I was pushing Ernie's car to its limit.

I had just passed the turn-off to Wyong when my phone rang. I popped it on speaker. "Jane? You find Sophie?"

"I thought like I was someone being chased. You know, used my brain. Maybe you don't know how."

"To the point, Jane?"

"She's going to want to be in a crowd, not on her own somewhere. I doubt she'd come back here, and since there's no match playing at Blue Tongue

Stadium, there's nothing happening in Gosford."

"To the fucking point, Jane." I slowed and pulled onto the shoulder. "Have you found her or not?"

"I know where she is. I don't have her eyes on her at this minute."

I looked in the rear-view mirror. No traffic. "Where? I'll be there as fast as I can push this car."

"I pulled into the Tuggerah station and saw her heading toward the shopping centre. It's open for a couple more hours. Maybe she's meeting someone there who can hide her."

I crossed the three lanes of the southbound freeway and hit the grass median at about 60. "She's got family in Newcastle. Don't know about any friends in Tuggerah. But I'll be there in about fifteen minutes. Less. I just passed the off-ramp."

"Next exit is ten minutes down the road, Mac. I'll head to the shopping centre and see if I can track her."

"Fuck the next exit." I hung up and came out of the median hitting the northbound pavement and floored it. I might end up owing Ernie a new car after this.

The Wyong exit to the Tuggerah mall was less than a kilometre in front of me now. I hit it at something north of 140 and had to slow quickly or overshoot into the rhubarb.

A few minutes later, I was parked in the massive shopping centre parking lot. It was getting close to closing time. The busiest place would be near the theatres. I ran up the escalator, barging a young couple to one side and yelling an apology as I hit the top. A crowd milled in the lobby, either waiting to get in, or blabbing about what they just saw. The last movie I saw in a theatre that was any good was Donnie Darko. Most of the stuff today is -- ah, shit. I'm starting to sound like my old man.

Terry and Jane did not blend in well with the crowd. They made a point of looking at each person in the face, even the guys, which made no sense.

I took a step back into a corner and surveyed the crowd, trying to pick out security. They were easy to find. They were wearing polyester suits, and their radios were on a loop in the small of their backs, so it looked like they were reaching for a gun when they were just turning up the volume for the obvious earbuds. And they didn't appear to be paying much attention to anyone except each other.

And then Sophie walked in front of me. I grabbed her by the wrist and pulled her into the alcove. "Why'd you come here? I thought you were going to Gosford."

"Jesus, Mac. You scared the crap out of me." She pulled her head back a bit and squinted at me. "Hang on. How did you find me? I was trying to be completely unpredictable."

"I'm good. Very good. Let's get the hell out of here. We can talk in the car on the way back home." I stepped out and gave Jane a quick wave, gave her a thumbs up and Sophie and I made a beeline for the exit.

Chapter Thirty-Five

"So, Sophie. Ready to finish this?"

She craned her neck to look in the back of the car. "Whose car is this?

"Ernie's. He wasn't using it."

"You're abusing that guy."

"He knows it. Doesn't seem to mind." I left the parking lot and pointed towards the highway back home.

Sophie looked at me for a spell, not talking. I sat her out. "What happened to me hiding out until this all blows over?"

"Jackson has put the word out to find you. And

me. Both of us. He's looking south. And you're not in Gosford, so maybe you picked up on it."

"Gosford Station was swarming with police. So I crossed the platform and headed back north. Figured they would be looking farther south, also."

I nodded in appreciation. "Smart move. Jackson thinks you know something."

"So where are we going?"

"A face-off." I hit the freeway northbound and floored it, pushing Ernie's little car to its limits. "Clean this shit up, once and for all."

"Sounds like you haven't put a lot of thought into this. He's going to kill us."

I smiled. "He's going to try." I cruised north for a few minutes, then took the exit to Morisset. Pulled over and took my phone out. "But I need a little bit of insurance first."

I dialled a number from memory and waited. He'd still be in the office. He was always in the office.

After five rings, when I was about to hang up and try to conjure a Plan B, he answered. "Superintendent Thomas speaking."

"Josh? Mac here. I understand some of your boys

have been looking for me."

"I need you to come in."

"I'd love to come in, but I don't trust you guys. You know anyone named Dave Thompson?"

"Who? What's this got to do with anything? Mac, there's an arrest warrant out for you for Jimmy's murder. You need to come in."

I drummed my fingers on the steering wheel. "Let's work toward that. I need some assurances that you'll listen to what I have to say before you let that cretin Jackson near me. One of us will kill the other before the day is through."

"You'll have your chance in court."

I punched the inside panel of the door with the side of my fist and shook the pain out of my hand. "Josh, buddy, this ain't going to court. Jackson'll kill me before he lets that happen." I looked across the car at the passenger seat. "And I want protection for Sophie Patterson, too."

Silence on the line. Not even Kenny G. I took the phone from my head and looked at the screen, then plugged a headset in and popped the buds in my ears. "You still there, Josh?"

I heard a click on the line.

"How is Jackson involved in this?" Asked Josh.

"Grab George Harris, the new bank manager. I've got him on tape admitting to some of what I'm being accused of. Jackson is in on it, too. I'm sure the office jockey will crack and give up Jackson."

Josh sighed on the other end of the line. "I've got no reason to pick him up. None. He's an upstanding citizen."

I patted my pockets. "Hang on a second." I pulled out the inventory list I'd snagged from the bank, smoothed it on my leg and took a picture of it with my phone. Then I selected one of the photos I took from the back room and sent the two of them to his mobile. "You still there?"

"Yeah."

"Your mobile number still the same?"

"Hasn't changed in over ten years. Why?"

"Good. I've just sent you two different photos of the cash bag log from the transfer that went missing. If Harris were on the up and up, these two lists would be identical. One was signed off in the back room in front of me, and the other was signed by the guard.

Different numbers. Different moneybags. Same signature." I checked the time on the phone. "I've been on the phone too long. I've got people to see."

There were a few clicks on the line, then, "Is Sophie with you?"

"Jesus. I *was* on too long, wasn't I? One more thing. Your guys picked up a couple of surfer dude thugs earlier this evening. They're dead in the surf off the beach where you found Jimmy. Jackson shot them. There should be enough circumstantial evidence to tie him to it. Plus, I've got him on tape doing it."

I stabbed the call off and tossed the phone in the centre console.

"What was that about?"

"I think we need to get to the station and turn ourselves over to Josh. Better deal with him than duck bullets from Jackson."

"You know what you're doing?"

"I sure hope so. I've known Josh since I was a teenager. I trust him. I trust him more than any other man in the state." I put the car in gear and pulled the car from the curb. "You agree?"

She nodded. "To the police station and see Josh. And I know who has the million dollars."

"Me too. I still don't know how——" I yanked the wheel to the right to avoid a black ute bearing down on us. "Shit. Jackson."

I floored it, pushing the small engine into the redline region. The front wheels spun on the pavement, almost wrenching the steering wheel from my hands. I miss rear-wheeled drives cars.

I glanced in the rear-view mirror and saw the ute fishtail as it U-turned and started chasing. "Hang on. This is going to get——"

A sharp report followed almost immediately by the sound of a shot hitting the back of the car. "Son of a bitch. The arsehole just shot the car."

Sophie gripped the dash and leaned into the sharp corner as I hauled the wheel to the left. "Ernie's going to be pissed."

I smiled at her. "If that's the biggest worry you have, you're tougher than I thought you were."

She winked and shifted her weight as I straightened the car. A second shot took out the driver's side mirror.

I looked at the shattered glass. "Shit. This is getting nuts."

Three more shots rang out. Sophie ducked and held on as I wrenched the wheel to the right, ducking down a small side road. She grimaced. "Where's a cop when you need one?"

"Good question." I grabbed my phone from the centre console and punched out 0-0-0, and stuck the phone between my shoulder and ear.

"Emergency Services. What is the nature of your—"

The truck slammed into the rear end of the car, dislodging the phone and spilling it to the floor.

"Fucking beautiful. Well, we're almost there anyway." I looked over at Sophie who was hanging on to the 'holy shit' handle above the door with both hands. "Having fun yet?"

The station, a one-story brick building taking up half a block on the main drag, was just ahead. I checked the rear-view mirror. The ute was close, and there was no way I would outrun it. I held the wheel and put on the emergency brake, turning the wheel and skidding to a stop in front of the station. "Out,

out, out." I grabbed my phone from under the seat and followed her.

We ran up the sidewalk and the front steps to the station. I had my hand on the front door of the station when the truck stopped, and a shot splintered brick above my head.

I turned and pulled Sophie behind me. "Jesus Christ, Jackson. Are you fucking insane? You're out of control."

Jackson stood in the Weaver stance, both hands on his sidearm. "Run. Please. I can shoot you and be done with it."

A black and white police car stopped, and two uniforms got out with their guns drawn. I held up my hands. "Hang on, you two. This is the guy who robbed the bank. With Harris' help. Jackson's got a sweet mill sitting in the bank."

Jackson barked at the uniforms. "Arrest him. Jesus. What are you waiting for?"

I took my phone out of my back pocket and pushed it back into Sophie's hands. I continued talking to Jackson. "That one account is in the name of Dave Thompson. Who do you think that might be,

Jackson?"

I stepped forward and waved my phone behind me, willing Sophie to take it. She grabbed it and ran into the station. "Your son's name is Dave, right? I hope his arm is okay, by the way. Dave, Tom's son. Dave Thompson. You guys and your stupid fucking aliases. If you had used something like Dick Smith or Harvey Norman, I'd have never figured it out." I shook my head and smiled at him. "Vanity. Soph checked the Dave Thompson signature card, and it looks remarkably similar to yours, Tommy boy."

Jackson gripped his handgun even tighter and slowly walked toward me. I took a couple of steps back into the front door of the station just as Sophie ran through it with Josh in tow. She slammed into my back, drove me forward, and I fell at Jackson's feet.

He straddled my legs and cuffed me, then dragged me to my feet. "Jesus, you've got a big mouth." He leaned in close and whispered in my ear. "You won't make it to trial, mate. I'll drop you in the ocean with a bullet in your head before that happens."

The wound on my arm opened in the ruckus.

"You're getting my blood on your shirt, Jackson."

Jackson pulled me around and faced me in the general direction of the precinct. Josh Thomas held up my phone and waved one of the uniforms over. "Bag this." He turned to Jackson. "Take the cuffs off him. Now."

"Boss, it's a good collar. This guy is good for the bank job."

"Take them off. Now."

Jackson hesitated for a minute, then grumbled something and removed them. "Jesus."

"Excellent. Now let's go into my office and talk. Harris is telling me a pretty interesting story. Most of it I already heard, thanks to Mac's phone. You've got some explaining to do."

Chapter Thirty-Six

It was good to be clear of it. Finally. The paperwork took weeks, and I was officially a person of interest until this morning. Harris had the money spread across the fourteen accounts, plus Jackson's and they were planning on transferring it offshore. The notification of an audit screwed up the timing for them. He had to devise a plausible way of getting four and a half mill off the books, and the 'robbery' was the best he could come up with.

I cubed the chicken and dropped it in the pan with olive oil and some nice Tuscan seasoning. Lincoln let out a small "woof" and padded into the kitchen. "No chicken for you, fatty. You're on a diet." He looked at me with his chocolate Border Collie eyes and managed to make me feel guilty. "Oh, dammit." I pulled a piece from the frying pan and tossed it to him. He caught it on the full, wagged his tail and loped back to the sofa, which he'd made his own.

The television in the living room was on Sky News. The headlines at the top of the hour came on. I walked to the front of the TV with a head of cos lettuce in my hand.

"Tonight at 7:00 on Seven, an update on the bank robbery and murder that has the bank manager and a local police officer in jail awaiting trial."

I smiled and turned off the TV. "Excellent." I returned to the kitchen area and finished chopping the lettuce and cherry tomatoes. I make a mean Caesar salad.

I sliced the boiled eggs, added them, the chicken and croutons to the bowl and shaved in some Parmesan. I hadn't cooked like this in years. It felt good.

I lit the candle on the centre of the table just as

someone knocked on the door. Lincoln let out another quiet "woof" and padded to the door. I followed and opened it to Sophie, hair up in a ponytail and wearing a summer dress and sandals. It was finally getting warm out.

She ignored me and squatted down to pat Lincoln. "You got your dog back."

"Lincoln. Also answers to Linc, Lynx and, apparently, Linky-poo, thanks to Jane. Terry really is allergic to dogs, and Jane prefers the person to the mutt. Fine by me."

She gave Lincoln a hug and stood and sniffed. "Hmm. What smells so good?"

Lincoln pushed his nose into her hand, looking for more attention. She scratched him under the chin and followed me into the kitchen.

"Seriously. It smells good."

"That's the apple-rhubarb crumble. Warm chicken Caesar first." I took Sophie into my arms. "You know, it was nice having all that money in my bank account, even if it was just for a short time."

"I got a call from Terry on the way over. He's the manager now. Turns out there was a reward. Five per cent."

"Two twenty-five isn't bad. I could live with that."

Sophie leaned back in my arms and looked up at me. "Who says it's yours? I found the money."

"You only looked because I told you to."

She interrupted me with a kiss. "I'll split it with you, okay?" She looked around my apartment with a frown on her face.

"Better than the Wayfarer, right?"

She looked up at me and smiled. "It'll do."

ABOUT THE AUTHOR

Tony McFadden is a Canadian now happily living in
Australia, a land with very little snow, writing near the
beach whenever possible.

You can find him on the interwebs at
www.TonyMcFadden.net,

Also by Tony McFadden

Matt's War
Daly Battles: The Fall of PyongYang
Target: Australia

G'Day LA
G'Day USA

Book 'Em
Family Matters
Unprotected Sax
(with Charles McFadden)

Have Wormhole, Will Travel
Killing Time

A Step Too Far (A Mac-D Mystery)
Hunter / Prey (A Mac D Mystery)

The Murder of Jeremy Brookes
Number Fifteen

Batteries Not Included
Broken
Dead Tomorrow
Under the Shadows

www.ingramcontent.com/pod-product-compliance
Lightning Source LLC
Chambersburg PA
CBHW010301100726
47904CB00011B/2692